Yesterday's News

SAM CHEEVER

~SC~

Antiques can be a dangerous business. Especially when you're dealing with a desperate politician, a sexy ex-cop, and a couple of "spirited" companions.

Anna Yesterday owns Yesterday's Antiques in small town USA. When she finds an old newspaper clipping lining the drawer of an antique dresser, she realizes she's never heard the heart wrenching story of abuse and suicide detailed on the yellowed newsprint. So she starts to dig, and her sleuthing exposes an ugly cover-up that casts the residents of Crocker, Indiana into danger and intrigue, and leaves them with a corpse.

GLOSSARY

Since Joss and Bess are from America's colorful past, I thought it might be good to provide a glossary of the colloquialisms they use in the text of this book. Some of them don't require explanation. I haven't included those, but the more interesting ones certainly could use a little clarification. Even within context, the meanings of some of the following terms can't be easily ascertained.

Absquatulated: to disappear

All-overish: uncomfortable

Backing and filling: waffling

B'hoy: rowdy boy, ruffian

Cap the climax: beat all

Catchin' a weasel asleep: referring to something that's unlikely

Chirk: cheerful

Codfish aristocracy: a contemptuous term for rich business people

Coot: a simpleton

Cotton to: take a liking to

Fix one's flint: to settle a matter

Fyst: A worthless dog, a mongrel

G'hal: rowdy girl, ruffian

Gotham City: New York City

Grab the little end of the horn: short end of the stick

Grum: gloomy

Hang up the fiddle: give up

Hoister: manipulator, operator

Hornswoggle: cheat

Humbugs: deceptions

Knock into a cocked hat: to knock senseless

Necktie sociable: hanging

Pucker: state of irritation

Puke: A person from Missouri

Right smart: a large quantity

Rip-snortin': An impressive person

Saw the elephant: see it all clearly

sharper: a crook

Shut pan: shut up

Swan: swear

Wake snakes: raise a ruckus

Wrathy: to be angry

CHAPTER ONE

Yesterday, 1964

Tatty Baker crouched down behind a large rock and watched the two white men argue. The big man was wearin' a smooth white shirt under his 'spenders and dark pants that had a crease in 'em sharp as a butcher's knife. The other man was dressed far less grand, in dingy pants with uneven cuffs and a yellowed shirt that was smudged with something dark. He seemed to be gettin' the worst of the arguin'. The little guy just stood his ground while the other man poked a thick finger into his scrawny chest over and over, and he didn't punch back. Tatty would have. In his opinion, there was nothin' worse than somebody pokin' that bone. Tatty knew from experience. He had brothers.

Tatty was too far away to hear what the men were arguing about. The big man had his face close to the other guy's and was talking real low. Tatty could just hear the rumble of his deep voice as he gave the other guy what for.

Tatty had seen the men before, downtown. They worked in the red brick building on Main Street and had somethin' to do with tellin' stories. Least that's what Tatty's mama told him. Tatty always thought it would be a fine way to earn your supper...tellin' stories. He got lots of practice doin' that

3

every day when his mama asked him where he'd been when he was s'posed to be doin' his chores.

Tatty figured someday he'd wear a smooth white shirt and fancy pants and tell stories to earn his keep. In the meantime, he wanted to know what the two men was doin' out in the middle of nowhere. And he really wanted to know what those big stacks of paper was. The small man had unloaded 'em from a dented pickup truck and dumped 'em in the middle of the mayor's field.

Tatty knew he shouldn't be there. His instructions was to just leave the jar of peaches with mayor Bethesda's maid, Wilma, and get on back home, fast as ever. But Tatty had a natural curiosity and when he spotted the truck and the two men he'd just had to hunker down and check it out. Mama always told him his nosiness was gonna land him right in the devil's lap some day. But Tatty liked to think he had a nose for trouble. He of a certain created enough of it himself.

That's why Tatty knew them men was doin' something bad out there.

So he crouched behind that rock and watched. A few minutes later the big man gave the little guy a final poke and turned away. He headed toward the truck and stopped, turning to call out, "…and make sure it all burns. Or we'll both be out of a job tomorrow."

Tatty's eyes widened. They was gonna burn the stacks of paper. He sure did wish he had a stick and a frankfurter with him. His mouth watered on the thought as the man lit a match and dropped it onto the stacks of paper. He waited and watched for a minute, until the stacks flared into a hardy flame and a dense coil of smoke slipped silently upward, toward a cloudless sky lit by a near-full moon.

Tatty's nose twitched on the scent of burning paper and he sighed. His brother Will would have loved to see the fire. It was a dandy. The men climbed inside the truck and drove off, bumpin' and rollin' on the uneven turf of the freshly turned cornfield.

After a minute, Tatty gave in to the urge to move closer to the fire. He picked up a long stick and carried it with him, hoping to have some fun pokin' at the burning embers to make 'em flare. But as he approached, a soft wind slipped across the field, spicy with the scent of rain, and a hunk of the paper broke loose and flew in his direction.

Tatty dropped the stick and caught the paper, swearing like he shouldn't as the smoldering edge burned the top of his arm. The words on the paper were small and black and perfect, and Tatty had never seen anything so wonderful in all his life.

Stories.

He clasped the slightly charred treasure to his chest and started to run, determined to take the stories home to Mama. She liked to read 'em after dinner at night. The thought made Tatty's smile widen, showing a full mouth of white teeth as he ran through the dark night.

Brilliant white, like the big man's shirt.

Present Day

"You want me to move this to the back?"

Anna Yesterday looked up from her pile of receipts and nodded. "Thanks, Pratt. I need to clean it out and repair that one drawer before we put it on the floor."

Pratt Davies was Anna's new assistant at Yesterday's Antiques and they were still dancing around each other, trying to find a rhythm that worked. Anna hadn't decided if he was going to work out. It wasn't that Pratt was inept, lazy, or even annoying. In fact, he was as far from all of those things as a person could get. But Pratt was new in Crocker, Indiana, and nobody knew much about him. And Anna couldn't quite shake the idea that Pratt was almost too perfect. At well over six feet, with dark brown hair that he wore military short, golden brown eyes, thick lashes, a strong nose, a broad jaw, and full lips, Anna found his presence in her antiques store more than a little discomfiting. He was smart and intuitive and she had to wonder why he'd settle

5

for an assistant's position in an antique store, in a tiny town in the Midwest.

Pratt strapped the small dresser onto a hand truck and pulled the strap tight, the muscles in his arms bulging enticingly as he tilted it back to move it. Anna's chin fell off her hand and she straightened guiltily.

"That boy's trouble you know."

Anna jumped and turned at the sound of the husky drawl. Josselin Zebediah was perched on the bookshelf behind her desk, his sexy, dark blue gaze fixed on her with more than a little irritation. She glared at him. "What have I told you about sneaking up on me?"

Joss straightened his long, long legs and stood, tipping the well-worn cowboy hat down on his forehead. "I don't sneak." He moved across the store in large, scuffed boots and stood watching Pratt roll the antique dresser into the back room. "The boy's a grifter. He'll hornswoggle ya faster'n I can spit tobacco into that pan over there."

Anna sighed. They'd had the very same conversation at least a dozen times in the week since Pratt had started working at Yesterday's Antiques. She was growing weary of it. "You don't chew tobacco." Turning back to her paperwork, Anna tried to ignore Joss. "We've had this discussion several times, Joss. I refuse to have it again."

Joss didn't give up easily. "You know nothin' about that boy. He could kill ya cold as a wagon tire in your sleep."

"I don't sleep in the store."

"That wouldn't stop a varmint like him." Joss was as overprotective as a well-trained dog, only with a bigger bite. But above all he was a friend and he cared for her.

"I know what I need to know about him. He's from Missouri. And he used to be a cop."

"A puke. Figures."

A cool breeze wafted past and Anna reached for the sweater on the back of her chair without looking up from the receipts. The sweater settled over her shoulders without her ever touching it. She looked up with a smile. "Thanks, Joss."

He smiled back and Anna felt the familiar twang of desire low in her belly. Joss Zebediah was an old-fashioned man, with a cowboy's manners and an old-world way of looking at things. With his craggy, down-on-the-range good looks and husky voice, he was also sexy as heck.

If he were alive Anna would jump his bones in a heartbeat.

Pratt walked back into the store, wiping his big hands on his jeans. He had a spider web trailing off one sleeve and a smear of dust on his lightly stubbled cheek. Anna had to clench her hand to keep from reaching out and wiping the dust off his face. "All set. I put it next to your worktable. I think that bottom drawer's swollen shut though. I tried to pull it out to see if I could fix it and it won't come loose. I didn't want to break it so I didn't put any muscle into it." He grinned and Anna's stomach fluttered. She threw Joss a guilty look and sure enough, he'd pushed his hat back on his head and arched a judgmental blond eyebrow at her. She gave him a quick frown. "Thanks Pratt. I'll put a heat lamp on it for a while. It's probably swollen from being down in old Mrs. Baker's cellar. You can go if you want. I'll be closing up soon anyway."

Pratt chewed the sexy fullness of his bottom lip. "You sure? I can finish cleaning out those whiskey barrels before I leave."

Anna picked up the receipts and slipped them into the top drawer. She'd finish going through them in the morning, before she opened the store. It was quieter then, with fewer distractions wearing snug jeans over muscular thighs and a truly stupendous backside. "No, you go on home. I won't be ready to put those out until next week anyway. I'm going to sell them with pots of flowers and the flowers won't be delivered until Monday."

"Oh. Okay." Pratt looked toward the door but didn't move.

Anna watched him, wondering why he hesitated.

"You want me to toss his ass out?" Joss asked helpfully.

Ignoring the cowboy, Anna asked, "Is there something else, Pratt?"

He shoved his hands into his pockets and sighed. "I'm sorry. It's just that...well..." He smiled a little sadly. "I hate going back to the hotel and sitting around by myself all night. It's lonely."

Anna's heart broke a little. She could only imagine how difficult it would be to start over in a new town, not knowing anyone. "It's Friday night. You could go over to Ray's. I hear it can get pretty interesting there on the weekends." She smiled, hoping he wouldn't take her words as a dismissal. But she was tired and still had stuff to do. The sooner she could shoo him out and lock the door behind him, the sooner she could finish up and go have a long, hot bath in her claw-footed tub.

"I was wondering if you'd like to go have a bite to eat. I hate to eat alone."

"The boy's crazy as a loon."

Anna threw Joss a glare. "Tonight? Oh, Pratt, I'm really tired tonight. And to tell you the truth I don't think it would be a good idea. Since we work together." Anna hated the look that flashed through his eyes but she didn't believe in obfuscating. She was a straight up, honest sort of person. She'd learned the hard way that honesty was less hurtful in the long run than a well-meaning lie.

"Oh, okay. Well, then I'll see you in the morning."

" 'Night, Pratt.

"Dash it! I thought he'd never leave."

"Shush, Joss. I don't know why you don't like him. He's a very nice young man."

Joss snorted. "Young man. I think he's older than you are. And don't you ever wonder why he's here? Crocker, Indiana ain't exactly Gotham City."

The cowboy had used that term before so Anna knew he was referring to New York City. She shrugged, unwilling to let him know she'd had the same doubts. He was already insufferable where Pratt was concerned. "That's his business. I'm just glad to have him. He's a good worker. Lock up for me, will you? I need to get tags on all that jewelry in the back tonight. It's going on sale tomorrow."

"You got it, darlin'."

Joss flipped a hand toward the front door and the deadbolt slipped home. A twitch of his fingers turned the *Open* sign to *Closed*.

Anna headed toward the large room at the back of the store where she worked on the antiques before she put them on the floor to sell. As soon as she walked through the door she knew trouble was waiting for her.

Trouble at Yesterday's Antiques wore cloying perfume and had a snotty attitude. At the moment, trouble was sitting on top of the dresser Anna needed to work on and was trying on the jewelry she needed to tag. Anna pasted a smile that she didn't feel on her face. "Hey, Bess. How are you tonight?" She grabbed the heat lamp off her work table and settled it in front of the dresser, focusing the light on the swollen bottom drawer.

The woman turned a clown-like countenance toward Anna, frowning. "Pshaw! I'm in a fine pucker. You've been keepin' Jossy tied up all day and there's been nobody to wake snakes with."

Anna moved to the sink against the far wall and turned on the water, soaping up her hands while she fought the need to respond to the crabby poltergeist with a snarky remark. Bess hated Anna and the store. It was just her bad luck, and everybody else's, that something of hers got caught up in the place a couple of centuries earlier and she couldn't leave. Anna had been afraid to search for the binding item for fear she'd open the front door and chuck it into the back of a passing truck if she found it.

Maybe a road trip would do the cranky saloon girl some good.

Drying her hands carefully, Anna responded patiently, "I haven't been monopolizing Joss, he goes where he goes. Maybe if you were nicer to him…"

"Don't lay out your humbugs to me, Missy! I swan you use your wiles on him. You've got that poor cowboy backing and filling until he can't find his hat with his left hand while holding it in his right."

Anna stood with her arms crossed over her chest, just staring at her unwelcome visitor. She'd almost grown used to the woman's colorful way of talking…even enjoyed it most days…but she was not currently having one of those days. "You know as well as I do that Joss has a mind of his own, Bess." Anna held out her hand, palm up. "Now give me that necklace, I need to tag it for sale."

Bess flicked her pale, slim fingers and the necklace flew toward Anna's face. Fortunately, Anna had been expecting it and caught the heavy gold piece before it hit her nose. "Why don't you go help Joss close up the store?"

Bess's emerald colored eyes widened under the bright blue of her saloon girl eye shadow. She pursed heavily stained red lips and disappeared in a puff of clove-scented air. Anna smiled. Joss was gonna kill her for sending Bess his way, but it would be worth it for a few minutes of peace. She settled herself at the long wooden table and picked up her tags and marking pen. Reaching into the overflowing box of antique jewelry, some real and some kitschy fakes, Anna put the cranky ghost out of her mind and set to work.

An hour later she realized the store was unusually quiet and became concerned. It was never good when her two resident specters were quiet. If they weren't fighting, Bess was usually pounding on the old Steinway Anna kept at the back of the store, screeching like a mouse in the clutches of an eagle.

Needing an excuse to get up and stretch anyway, Anna stood and went to investigate. She opened the door into the store and stopped, amazed at the sight that greeted her. Joss was sitting behind the counter; his well-worn cowboy hat tipped back on his head and a thoughtful expression on his face. Bess was perched on the tall stool on the other side, her impossibly long legs crossed and the lace of her petticoats showing as she kicked one foot and examined her nails, obviously waiting for Joss to make his move.

The antique chess set Anna had brought into the store a week earlier was settled between them. As Anna watched, Joss lifted a finger and a rook skittered sideways and stopped. He gave Bess an expectant look and she bent to study the board.

Joss winked at Anna. She grinned and mouthed, "thank you", quietly stepping backward and closing the door. She owed Joss big time for keeping Bess occupied and giving her some peace.

With a sigh she looked at the box of remaining jewelry and suddenly couldn't face it. Instead, she decided to tackle the drawer on the dresser. The heat lamp had done its work. The drawer was unstuck but still sticky. Pulling carefully, Anna was able to wrench it open after a couple of tries.

"Gotcha!" she exclaimed happily. The sour smell of old wood wafted out to make her nose twitch and Anna looked inside. Other than a few buttons and a yellowed old newspaper, the drawer was predictably empty. There was an old, black sock with a hole in the toe in the middle drawer and a yellowed hankie in the top one. Anna carefully extracted the paper and the forgotten items and set them aside. She grabbed a rag and some polish and ran the rag quickly over the dresser. With the dust gone, it was easier to examine the few scratches in the front and top of the sixty-year-old piece of furniture. Anna decided she could get by with a scratch treatment and a good polish, rather than sanding it down and refinishing it. The dresser was in surprisingly good shape.

Pleased with her discovery she stood, stretched, and yawned. Her eyes were gritty and her back hurt from bending over the jewelry for so long. Casting a guilty look at the remaining baubles, Anna briefly considered finishing the job of marking them. In the end she decided they could wait until the morning. Saturday mornings were always slow and her bubble bath was calling to her.

Anna threw the rag onto the table and the headline on the yellowed rectangle of newspaper caught her eye.

Mayor Bethesda Questioned in Housemaid's Rape

She blinked and found herself reaching for the newspaper, thinking it had to be some kind of joke. But the words beneath the headline were no joke. And the paper looked genuinely old. Anna read the account of the young woman who had worked in the mayor's mansion almost fifty years earlier. The girl had apparently caught the mayor's eye and paid a huge price for it. A chill slipped down her spine, along with a premonition of danger that made no sense.

"What you got, darlin'?"

Anna jumped, the newsprint slipping from her fingers. "Dammit, Joss! You scared the crap out of me."

She turned around and found him smiling unapologetically. "Boo."

Anna laughed, dropping the yellowed newsprint on the table and tapping the headline with her finger. "Do you remember this?"

Joss had been in Crocker, Indiana a long time. Ever since he'd been shot down in a gun battle in 1861, in the build-up to the Civil War. Crocker had been a collection of ramshackle buildings then, according to Joss, and he'd been buried, along with Bess, on the land where the antiques store now stood. The bodies had been moved decades earlier, when the town of Crocker had been built, but something of Joss's had remained behind, something that tied him inexorably to the store. Workers digging post holes in the back yard a couple of years earlier had uncovered Joss's cherished gun belt and holster, minus the gun. Sensing its value, Anna had cleaned it up and locked it in her safe on that very same day.

Joss appeared to her for the first time that night. Needless to say, he'd scared the daylights out of her then too.

"I ain't never seen that headline, darlin'. I remember that varmint Bethesda though, and his spoiled mongrel of a son. The little sharper used to come into the candy shop that was here then and hoist candy cool as you please. If the kid hadn't been the mayor's boy, I reckon he'd a ended up at a necktie sociable." Joss shook his head, looking properly appalled. "Kid would smile at the shopkeeper while he pulled foot with the goods. I reckon he knew she'd fear his daddy the mayor enough not to raise a ruckus."

Anna nodded. "You're talking about Mason Bethesda, right?"

"Crocker's current mayor? Less'n there's another skunk with the same name I'm guessin' it has to be. The Bethesdas been runnin' this town for a coon's age." He grimaced and Anna resisted the urge to commiserate. Once Joss got started on his long, long list of complaints about the Bethesdas, it took an act of nature to get him to stop. "Turns out I was right about that boy. He did grow up to be a hoister. He just done it in a suit."

Chuckling, Anna said, "I can't believe I've never heard of this before." She turned a speculative look toward her resident ghost. "And it's even more amazing you've never heard of it."

"Seems about as likely as catchin' a weasel asleep."

Weariness finally overcame curiosity and Anna decided to head home. "I'm locking this in the safe, Joss. I'll do some digging on it tomorrow." She grinned a wicked grin. "I doubt Mason Bethesda would want it known his daddy had been accused of rape."

Joss's husky laugh made Anna's stomach do an interested little flip. "I allow the spreadin' of that bit would make the mayor all-overish for sure."

CHAPTER TWO

Anna thought about the newspaper article over coffee the next morning. The more she thought about it the more curious she became. It seemed unlikely that an event like the one she'd read about could occur without anyone, ever, commenting on it during all the years of Mayor Bethesda's term in Crocker.

Not even his political opponents had brought it up.

Anna finally realized she wasn't going to be able to set her curiosity aside until she looked into it, so that was exactly what she'd do. She settled her coffee cup in the sink and rinsed it before grabbing her purse and keys and heading out the door. She checked the time on her phone and dialed the newspaper as she descended the stairs to her car.

The storefront newspaper office of the *Crocker Sun* opened at seven every morning. With any luck Doris Fetz would be in the mood to answer the phone. It rang several times before Anna gave up. Doris was apparently not in a talkative mood. Anna shook her head at the absurdity of putting a woman in the role of dealing with the public who really didn't like people.

She turned down Jackson Avenue and pulled her car into one of the parking slots in front of the *Sun*. The "Open" sign was on the door so Anna went inside, her arrival announced by the strident clang of the bell hanging over the door. The front room was empty. There was no gray-haired, grim-faced clerk manning the counter.

"Hello?"

Something crashed in the back room and a bouffed, blue-gray head popped around the door frame, a beady pair of dark brown eyes peering at her like shiny pebbles from under a lowered line of dense brown eyebrows.

Anna figured she was wasting her time but she plastered a sunny smile on her face. "Good morning, Doris."

The older woman's face darkened under the force of Anna's cheerfulness. "You startled me. I dropped the sugar all over the floor."

Anna held onto her smile by sheer force of will. "I'm so sorry. Can I help you clean it up?"

The bouffed head disappeared again and Anna listened to the sound of a spoon clanking against the side of a cup. A moment later Doris ambled out, a pink paisley mug clutched in her thick fingers. She stopped behind the counter and took a sip, apparently trying to pretend Anna wasn't there.

Unfortunately for her, Anna didn't intend to be ignored. "I wonder if you could help me find something."

Doris barely looked up, she took another sip of her coffee and settled it onto the counter. "I'm very busy, Anna."

Anna pursed her lips but managed not to start screaming. "I can see that. It won't take more than a minute. I just wondered if I could look through your old issues."

Doris cocked a wide hip and fixed her beady gaze on Anna. "Why would you want to do that?"

"I found something in an old dresser, a story about the mayor. I was interested in finding out more about it. It's from the sixties."

"What was it about?"

Doris's dark gaze widened as Anna told her. She shook her head. "You've got a fake paper. That never happened."

"So, you've never heard about this crime either?"

"Of course not. It never happened."

"The newspaper appears very real."

Doris turned away, heading for her desk with her coffee. "If that's all, I'm very busy."

Anna considered arguing with the crotchety clerk but realized it would do no good. Doris was not only cranky, she was as stubborn as an old mule. "Thanks anyway, Doris. Have a wonderful day."

Doris dropped into her desk chair with a long-suffering groan and appeared to forget Anna had ever been there. With no other choice open to her, Anna left.

She stood on the sidewalk outside the newspaper office and looked around. The morning that had started out warm and damp, with the smell of ozone in the air that promised rain, had turned smoldering in the few minutes it had taken her to deal with Doris.

Anna headed toward her car, fighting an unsettled feeling from the way things had gone with Doris. She really needed to look at the *Sun's* articles from that time. Her gaze slid to the pale brick of the tidy building across the street.

The library.

With a smile, Anna realized there was more than one way to get what she needed. She started across the street. A shrill horn blasted a foot from her elbow and she jumped, clutching her chest.

"Watch out, Miss Yesterday. Start seeing mopeds!"

Pierce Johnson puttered past, his unruly red hair flying around his head as his hands worked the brakes and gas on the handles of the small, bright yellow moped. As usual, he was dressed to tidy perfection, in dark brown slacks, ruthlessly creased and short enough to show pristine white socks with their tops folded an exact and careful inch from the top. He wore a golf shirt whose sleeves were also creased and the tails were tucked with manic precision into the white belt holding his trousers around a narrow waist.

"Sorry, Pierce!" Anna waved as he slid to a perfect stop at the stop sign, looking both ways with exaggerated care before moving forward.

Pierce was in his late teens and was autistic. He lived a very protected, coddled life with his mother on the North end of Main Street in Crocker. Anna had never met his father. She thought they were divorced. Part of the boy's daily regimen included a daily circle of the town on his moped, following the exact same route at the exact same time, wearing exactly the same kind of clothes in similar colors.

Anna knew from talking to Heather, his mother, that when Pierce got home at precisely nine fifteen every morning, he parked his moped in exactly the same spot in the garage and went inside to change into his "inside clothes" before having exactly two thirds of a cup of cooked oatmeal with three slices of banana and one cup of milk.

Anna wondered what it would be like to be that much in control of one's life. She'd lost control over hers years ago.

In fact, she might never have had it.

***

The library was cool as expected. Its relative silence compared to the busy street outside felt soothing. In the far corner, a local children's book author read excerpts from her latest book to a group of wide-eyed children sipping punch and nibbling on home-made cookies.

Anna lifted her hand to Denise Block, her friend from grade school and now a well-known author. Denise's bright voice never wavered from her story as she smiled at Anna and waved back.

Anna headed toward the microfiche room.

"Hello, Anna! Can I help you with something?"

She cringed inwardly and took a bracing breath before turning around. "Hi, Mike." The head librarian at the Crocker Library was a skinny, middle-aged man with slicked-over dark hair that always looked greasy. He peered at her through cloudy wire-rimmed glasses and fidgeted. Anna's gaze slipped to Denise and she found her friend laughing as she chatted up one of her audience. Denise's eyes widened when she met Anna's desperate gaze. A moment later Denise reached for her cell phone.

"I'm just going to the fiche room, Mike…"

"Oh good, I can come in there with you if you want. It's been way too long since you and I have had a chance to visit."

Anna started walking again, trying for a breezy response that really just came off as panicked. "I wish I could, Mike, but I…" Her cell phone rang. "I'm afraid I have to take this call." She ducked inside the fiche room, closing the door firmly in Mike's face and leaning against it.

Accepting the call, she exclaimed, "Oh heavens, you saved my life!"

"I'm workin' on it, darlin'."

Anna sucked air. "Joss? How the heck are you on the phone?"

"I'm a passel of 'lectric energy, darlin'. I can do considerable more. Do you need some help?"

"No. Sorry, I thought you were someone else. Her call must have bumped up against yours."

The horny librarian started pounding on the door. Anna braced herself in case he tried to blast through.

"Why are you calling me and…"

Ms. Yesterday!

Anna cringed. "What did you mean you're working on saving my life?"

"The biggest toad in the puddle came callin' this morning. The puke fixed his flint."

There was really only one big toad in Crocker. "The mayor?"

"Seems his eminence got a call from a little filly named Doris."

So fast? That was something. "Filly? Really, Joss, Doris is more bovine than equine."

His husky laugh was no less potent over the phone. "Makes no never mind. Throwin' the mayor's highfalutin ass out o' this store was the first thing Pratt the puke done that I cotton to."

"Why? Oh no…he threw the mayor out of my store?"

"Had to, darlin'. The man was havin' a conniption fit. I was ready to give him the old spectral whoop ass when the boy done my work for me."

The door at her back started to shift in its frame. *Really, Ms. Yesterday, I need to monitor you while you're using that machine. It's very delicate.*

"I have to go, Joss."

"Who's the mule's ass screaming at you, darlin'? You need me to come down there and knock him into a cocked hat?"

She grinned. "No. He's about ninety pounds after eating fruitcake, Joss. I think I can handle him."

"Okay then. You go on and get him, darlin'. I'll see ya in a bit."

Anna hung up and reached for the door handle. But Mike seemed to have been distracted away from his pursuit of access and amore. It was quiet again. Pressing her ear against the wood, Anna could hear Denise's bright, happy voice on the other side, coaxing Mike away from the door. She quickly moved to the microfiche, figuring she didn't have much time. She owed her friend a dinner for her help. Maybe two.

***

Anna left the library an hour later with nothing in hand. She'd found zero information about a rape in the mayor's mansion…or out of it for that matter. In fact, there was no news from that date that was tied to the big white house on the hill in any way. She'd searched nearly the entire year in both directions, just in case the paper she had in her possession had somehow gotten the date wrong. The only events of note for that entire year were the suicide of a young girl named Copper Smith and the opening of a new dry goods store in Crocker.

In fact, Gilfer's Dry Goods still existed. Only now it was a hardware store.

Gritty eyed and disappointed, Anna hot-footed it out of the library lest she run into Mike again, and headed to the store. It was a relief to open the back door and enter her cool, relatively quiet workroom.

Her peace didn't last long.

Something crashed to the floor at the front of the building. Anna threw her purse into her office, closed the door, and hurried to find out what was going on. By the time she reached the front shouts and screams vibrated the ceiling tiles above her head.

Stepping through the door, Anna took quick inventory. Pratt was on his knees, picking up shards of glass. Bess was perched on top of the counter, glaring at Joss with her pale, slender arms crossed over her considerable chest. And Joss stood before her, hat tilted back on his head, feet planted wide in battle stance, and an accusing finger pointed in Bess's direction as he reamed her out. "You did that on purpose, g'hal…"

"Don't get all wrathy on me, Joss. I done the girl a favor…"

"Shut pan!"

Joss slid Anna a look that made her frown. What were her two resident ghosts keeping from her? "What's going on here?"

Pratt looked up from his task. "I'm sorry, Anna. I don't know how this happened. I was just cleaning the glass and it suddenly flew backward. I guess I don't know my own strength."

He looked so guilty Anna felt badly about having spoken harshly. Even though she'd been speaking to the spooks rather than him. Sometimes it was hard to remember nobody else heard or saw the ghosts. "It's okay, Pratt. There's probably something wrong with one of the legs. Can you move it into the back when you get done with that and I'll have a look at it?"

Pratt glanced at the free-standing mirror, now missing most of its age-freckled glass, and frowned. She knew he was probably thinking the mirror wasn't worth much without its glass. He was wrong, it wouldn't be worth nearly as much as it was before, but the hundred-year-old frame was still worth something. "Sure. I'm really sorry, Anna."

"No worries, Pratt." She gave him a smile. "Really."

When he'd gone into the back room with the mirror she rounded on Joss and Bess, only to discover that the two rascals were gone. "We're not done with this," she murmured to the empty room. High above her head, the antique, crystal chandelier swung gently on a specter-induced breeze.

***

Hours later, Anna was dropping protective bags over several antique ball gowns when Pratt came out of the workroom, rubbing his hands on a rag. He caught her eye and smiled, and Anna experienced a quick jolt of awareness that made her uncomfortable. She quickly turned away, hanging the last bag over the rack beside the counter and handing the receipt to her pretty young customer. "There ya go, Gretta. You're going to have the prettiest wedding Crocker's ever seen."

The young woman sighed. "I hope so. I'm exhausted already and I still have a thousand details to figure out."

Smiling, Anna patted her arm. "From what I've seen you've nailed the most important ones. Your bridesmaids are going to be stunning in these." She jerked her head toward the dress bags.

She was rewarded for her support with a bright smile. "Thanks." Gretta Longdon was marrying a young professor from nearby Indiana University. Brock Styles taught history at the school and Gretta had thought it would be fun to have a historical wedding.

Anna looked at Pratt as he approached. "Pratt, could you help Gretta get these dresses to her car?"

"It would be my pleasure." He turned his thousand-watt smile on the unsuspecting Gretta and the young woman actually blushed with pleasure.

Anna felt a jolt of something that might have been jealousy. If the idea weren't completely ridiculous. "Thanks, Gretta. Good luck with the wedding."

She watched them walk out the front door and then looked around. It was suspiciously quiet in the store and had been all day. "Joss?"

She waited, listening, but there was nothing. Anna frowned. It wasn't like Joss to go missing for even a couple hours, let alone most of a day. The front door opened and Anna turned to Pratt. "All set?"

"She barely managed to fit them all in her car." He shook his head. "What did she need with all those ball gowns anyway?"

"She's throwing a period wedding."

Pratt stared at her, his sexy golden-brown eyes looking perplexed.

Anna laughed. "Historical. She's dressing her bridesmaids in them."

"Oh." He shook his head and grinned, obviously nonplussed by the vagaries of the female mind. "I guess that's a cool idea."

"Yeah. It really is. And it's very good for my business."

He nodded enthusiastically. *That* he understood.

"So, Pratt, what happened this morning with Mayor Bethesda?"

He blinked, looking confused, and Anna realized her mistake. He hadn't told her about the mayor's visit and he didn't know about Joss. He wouldn't believe it if he did, most likely. Her mind spun, trying to come up with a way to explain her knowledge. What she finally came up with was weak at best. "I ran into Pierce Johnson in town. He drives his moped past the store every morning and he saw the mayor yelling at you." She held her breath, hoping Joss hadn't exaggerated the altercation. Or that Pratt hadn't met the young autistic. Pierce wouldn't even look her in the eye when he spoke to her. The chances of him noticing anything strange in the store and then offering the information to her were slim to none.

"I was going to tell you…"

She shrugged. "I know. We've been busy today."

He looked relieved that she wasn't going to scream at him for throwing the mayor out of her store. "He demanded to see you and didn't believe me when I told him you weren't here. He was really hepped up about some newspaper article he said you had." Pratt fixed her with a worried look. "I don't think you should be alone when you see him."

"That bad, huh?"

"Yeah. He wouldn't tell me what it was about but I got the impression the article wasn't something he wanted seen." Pratt stared at her, clearly wanting her to explain. Anna didn't think it was a good idea to spread the information from the news article around until she figured out what was going on.

"Thanks, Pratt. I'm sorry you had to go through that."

"I'm just glad you weren't here. And if he comes back, you'll want to make sure I'm in the room with you. Just in case."

Anna nodded and turned away, feeling guilty she hadn't confided in Pratt after he'd taken one for the team, so to speak. She told herself she'd explain it to him later, as soon as she figured it out herself. In the meantime, if a simple request to view old records at the newspaper had the mayor stomping into Yesterday's Antiques making angry demands, it might be safer for Anna to keep the news close until she knew what she was dealing with.

Safer for everyone but her anyway.

CHAPTER THREE

Rain beat a constant staccato on the windows of the store, occasionally driven into the glass by a burst of harsh wind. Anna sat on her stool behind the counter, leaning on her elbows and watching it come down. Rain always made her contemplative.

"A penny for your thoughts?"

She jumped and turned to Joss, frowning.

"I didn't sneak, Missy. Your mind was up in them clouds."

Anna sighed. He was right. "I was just thinking." Actually, she'd been wondering about that story again. It had depressed her, thinking that the Bethesda family might have something as ugly as rape in its proverbial closet. Especially since Mason Bethesda had aspirations for higher political office.

If it was true and his father had never paid the price for the act, that would be a terrible thing for Mason's campaign. It was bad enough, in fact, that Anna was pretty sure Mason would do just about anything to keep it out of the news. His earlier behavior would seem to support her fear that he wasn't going to take kindly to her trying to uncover the truth.

"Hello? You back in them clouds?"

"I'm sorry, Joss. I was just thinking about that newspaper article. I haven't been able to find anyone who heard about the rape of this poor girl and the microfiche at the library didn't have anything on it at all."

He dropped his delectable butt onto the counter next to her and frowned. "Now that is a conundrum. Reckon it could be one of them false papers that show what happened on your birthday and such?"

"Not likely. Those papers *are* fake, but the news on them is always real. No. This is real newsprint. And the edges are singed, like somebody pulled it out of a fire."

Joss thought about this for a minute. Finally, he said, "Maybe Bess recollects somethin' about it."

Anna had forgotten about Bess. She liked to do that whenever possible. "You're right. I'll ask her. Thanks, Joss."

He reached out and pushed an errant curl behind her ear. Where he touched her, she felt tiny sparks but no heat and no skin. It always made her sad that she couldn't feel Joss. She figured touching Joss and having him touch her would be a life-changing experience.

"Now suppose you tell me what you and Bess were fighting about this morning."

Joss frowned and glanced guiltily toward the spot where the mirror had been. "Bess thought the puke had clapped eyes on her."

Anna nodded.

"He was cleaning that glass and she was standin' behind him. Of a sudden he flips around right quick like, with a face like a mackerel on a platter, and looks right at her. Bessy girl panics and gives the mirror the whammy to distract him."

Anna sighed. She realized Bess was trying to protect her, but she almost wished Pratt *did* know about her resident ghosts, it would make her life a lot simpler. That is, if he didn't run screaming from the place thinking she was loony. "Why didn't you just tell me?"

"Bess thought you'd get in a pucker about it. She don't think you cotton to her."

Anna was saved from having to respond to that little pool of quicksand when the front doorbell jangled.

Heather Johnson entered holding a stack of papers. She shook out a rainbow-hued umbrella and left it by the door. Pierce came through the door after her, taking care not to touch it with his fingers. He carried a pristine white hanky at all times so he didn't have to touch anything.

Heather explained that once, when he was a baby, she'd made the mistake of telling Pierce about germs. He'd latched onto the information and never let go.

The older woman smiled at Anna and waved. "Hello, dear. I wondered if you'd mind if I put a couple of flyers on your front windows."

"Good afternoon, Heather. Pierce."

The young man plucked at his shirt and studiously avoided her gaze. He moved through the store, checking out her inventory. "You have dirt on the floor, Miss Yesterday. You are a negligent shopkeeper."

Heather shushed him and smiled an apology. Lowering her voice, she told Anna, "He's in rare form today. Something's got him riled up but he won't tell me what."

"No problem. What do you have there?" Anna pointed to the flyers.

"I'm on Mayor Bethesda's Senate election committee. We're putting these flyers all over town."

The flyer Heather handed Anna had a big, smiling photo of the mayor in its center, with the headline, *Let's put Crocker on the Map – Elect Mason Bethesda for U.S. Senate*. The handsome Senator wore his trademark flag tie, which on anybody else would look cheesy. But somehow he made it work.

Anna tried not to cringe. The idea of Mason Bethesda going to Washington and making decisions about people's lives scared the crap out of her. "I try not to get involved in politics, Heather."

The other woman looked crestfallen. "Oh. Well, okay then."

Feeling guilty, Anna pointed to the light pole just outside her store. Fortunately, the rain had stopped and the sun was sneaking out from behind a thick bank of clouds. "Why don't you put one on the pole out there? That's just as good as my window, right?"

Heather turned and smiled. "You're right, Anna. Thank you." When Anna tried to hand her the flyer back, Heather refused to take it. "You keep that one, dear. We hope to have your vote come November." The woman actually winked at Anna. "Come on, Pierce. We're leaving."

Pierce was staring at an old bicycle. "I'm looking. I'll come out in a minute."

Heather sighed and started for the door. "I'll fetch him in a minute, Anna. You don't mind if he looks around, do you?"

"Of course not. Take your time."

Anna leaned her elbows on the counter again and dropped her chin into her hands, watching Pierce. "Do you like that bike?"

Pierce's hand moved toward the bike and then retreated, returning to pluck at his shirt. "It's got rust. Somebody was a careless bike owner."

Anna smiled. "It's very old."

"I like new things. This bike is old."

"Yes, it is." She watched him a moment longer. He looked at a few more things around the bike but he kept returning to it. "You know you could paint that and fix it up."

Pierce's hand plucked at his shirt and he examined the floor. "Make him stop looking at me."

Anna blinked, looking around. "Who?"

"Don't be coy, Miss Yesterday. The cowboy is rude. He's staring. He always stares."

Her mouth came open in a gasp. "You..." She glanced at Joss. "You can see the cowboy?"

"Is that a trick question, Miss Yesterday? Because I don't like tricks."

She looked at Joss again and he just shrugged.

"No. It's not a trick. The cowboy isn't used to people knowing he's there. He'll stop looking at you."

"That's silly. Of course people will know he's there. He's big, and his clothes need mending."

Anna grinned. "Is that so?"

"There's no call to be rude, boy." Joss frowned.

"It's not rude to tell the truth," Pierce explained patiently. "It's rude to stare."

"I was just wonderin' why you keep pluckin' at your shirt that way."

Pierce frowned and his face reddened. "I don't like to touch things. Unless they're my things."

"That ain't complete balderdash," Joss told him. He slid down from the counter and sauntered over to Pierce. "A body needs his own stuff. This here bike could be yours. Then you could touch it."

Pierce stared at Joss's big boots and plucked at his shirt. "Maybe. You should polish your boots."

Joss smiled at Anna. "I reckon I could do that…if you'll buy this bike.

"That's bribery or blackmail," Pierce told him. But he smiled. "I'll think about it. Goodbye, Miss Yesterday."

"Goodbye, Pierce."

Pierce's gaze flashed upward and then slid quickly away from Joss. "Goodbye, cowboy."

"See ya, hoss."

Pierce snorted. "I'm Pierce. You're hoss."

"No, you are."

Pierce snorted again and headed out of the store. He used the hanky to open the door and went outside to join his mother. She was talking to Denise Block. Anna waved at Denise as Joss rejoined her.

"What's wrong with that boy?"

"He's autistic."

"Oh, yeah, them painters can be a mite queer sometimes."

"Not artistic, autistic."

"What's the difference?"

The front door jangled again before she could respond. Denise came through the door with a wide smile. "Hey girl. You talking to yourself again?"

Anna resisted a glance at Joss as he chuckled. "Nobody else makes any sense."

Denise laughed. "Ain't that the truth. She stopped in front of the counter and dropped her duffel bag sized purse on its glass top. "What a day. It's only four o'clock and I'm exhausted."

"I hear ya."

Denise twisted her lips, obviously holding back a smile. "You created quite a ruckus in the library this morning."

Anna groaned. "It wasn't me creating the ruckus. That man is absolutely certifiable."

Denise laughed. "You won't get any argument from me. I'm just glad he has the hots for you and not me."

"Yeah. Lucky me."

Joss pushed his hat back on his head. "Is this somethin' I need ta address, darlin'?"

Anna widened her eyes at him. "Thanks for helping me out by the way. I owe you lunch."

"I'll take you up on that. What were you looking for in there anyway?"

Anna thought about it for a minute and then gave in to the temptation to show Denise what she'd found. "Can you come in the back room for a minute?"

Denise grabbed her bag. "Sure."

Anna looked at Joss.

"I'll keep an eye on things up here, darlin'."

She smiled her thanks and followed Denise to her workroom. She closed the door behind them and locked it, causing Denise's eyes to widen.

"This looks serious."

"It is." Anna headed for her cluttered little office in the back corner of the large space. "At least I think it is. I really haven't figured out what exactly it is yet."

"I'm intrigued."

Anna went to the large safe where she kept Joss's gun belt and all the other stuff she wanted to keep safe. She moved the box of junk she kept in front to hide it and knelt down to punch in her code. She opened the safe door and reached inside.

"Is that a gun belt and holster?"

Anna jumped guiltily and grabbed the folder she'd stuffed inside earlier, quickly closing the door. "Yes."

"What a strange thing to keep in the safe."

"It has…sentimental value," she told her friend with a smile. Handing the folder containing the yellowed newsprint to Denise, Anna said, "I pulled that out of an old dresser I got from Tatty Baker."

Denise opened the folder and quickly scanned the headlines, her pretty brown eyes widening with shock. "Holy, crap!"

"Yeah. That was my reaction too. Have you ever heard this story?"

Denise shook her head. "Never. I've never heard a hint of scandal connected to the Bethesdas. The men are all asses, but as far as I know none of them has gotten even a slap on the wrist legally. That's been Mason's biggest selling point during all his campaigns." She stiffened her shoulders and neck and lowered her voice to mimic the mayor's frequent commercials, "Mason Bethesda, the respectable, moral choice."

"Yeah, well, I think there might be some immoral skeletons in Mayor Bethesda's closet."

Denise shook her head. "If this were true somebody would know about it." She looked up. "Wouldn't they?"

"That's what I keep telling myself. But so far I haven't found anybody who knows about it."

"You checked with the newspaper?"

Anna snorted, "And got Mason Bethesda thundering into the store for my trouble."

"He came here?"

"When I was at the library trying to find this story on the fiche. My new assistant, Pratt handled him but I have a feeling he'll be back."

Denise handed the folder back to Anna and grinned. "I've seen your new assistant. If he needs somebody to take the sting of the mayor's rebuke away I'd be happy to help out."

Anna was surprised by the quick flash of jealousy her friend's playful offer caused. "Ha, ha. I'll let him know you're available to play doctor."

"I think I still have that nurse costume from last year's Halloween party."

Anna tucked the folder back into the safe and locked it. "You're a very bad girl, Denise Block."

"Ain't I just. It seems to me that if you want to know about that news story you should go to the source."

Anna frowned. "I did. I went to the paper…"

"Not *that* source. The source of the actual newspaper article. Tatty Baker."

Anna could have kicked herself. She blinked. Of course! "Denise, I owe you two lunches. You're a genius."

Her friend laughed. "I do try."

CHAPTER FOUR

Tatty Baker lived at the edge of town, where Main Street turned back into Highway 37, heading toward Kentucky. His small, brown house was simple but well kept, with fresh paint on the shutters and a riot of color from inexpensive annuals in simple flower boxes beneath the windows.

As she drove up the long and rutted driveway through the trees, Anna tried to remember what she knew of the family. Tatty's mother still lived in the house, along with Tatty. His brother Willard had owned the auto repair shop in town as long as Anna could remember, but he'd died of a massive heart attack the year before. Tatty's sister had moved North a decade earlier and rarely came to visit. Anna couldn't remember her name. It was something like Debra, or Delphine. Anna thought Tatty had had another brother but remembered something about him dying young.

She'd done business with the Bakers several times in the past. Whenever old Mrs. Baker needed a little extra cash that she couldn't make selling her beautiful quilts, delicious pies, or food she'd canned from the family's extensive garden out back, she'd sold Anna one of the family's well-kept pieces of antique furniture.

In fact it had happened so often lately that Anna had started to worry the family had only a couple of beds and a table or two left in their simple brown house.

A man came around the corner of the house as she stopped her car, and pulled a battered, old straw hat off his head. He leaned wearily on his hoe and watched her climb out of her little smart car, his brown eyes sparkling with humor. "Miss Yesterday, I'm waitin' for a bunch of them mijits to come pourin' out o' that car. Like at the circus."

Anna laughed. She was used to people making fun of her little car but she didn't care. It was cheap on gas and tons of fun to drive. "Don't knock it until you try it, Tatty. It's a lot easier to park in town than that monstrosity you drive."

His round face split in a grin, a perfect row of large white teeth giving the smile even more power than usual. "I'll stick to my truck, ma'am. You hit a good-sized crow with that thing and you'll be eatin' your grill."

She shook her head. "Your mama in?"

His smile dimmed considerably as he nodded. "I'm afraid it's not one of her better days today."

Old Mrs. Baker suffered from small, memory-eating strokes and it was never clear from day to day if she was going to be cognizant or not. "I wanted to ask her about that small dresser she sold me last week."

Tatty nodded. "Anything I can help you with?"

"Probably not. There was a piece of old newsprint lining the bottom drawer…"

"Yup, Mama never wastes a thing. Waste not, want not, she always says. And, Miss Yesterday she means every word of that and then some." He chuckled, straightening to take some of his weight off the hoe.

"I wanted to ask her if she remembered where she got it."

"I doubt she'd remember a thing like that. She might a' took it from the trash down behind the Quick Mart. Why you askin'?"

"It was a very old newspaper. There was a story in it that I hadn't seen before."

"Let's have a look at it then."

"I didn't bring it with me. It's very…delicate." Anna let him assume she'd meant the paper, though she'd left the paper in her safe for entirely different reasons.

Tatty nodded, his freckled brown brow furrowing. "Okay then. Sorry I can't help you none. But maybe if you come back tomorra Mama will be feelin' better."

Anna thanked him, spent a couple of minutes asking about the garden and what foodstuffs the family would be offering at the State Fair in August, and then climbed into her clown car and left. As she was driving down the long driveway, headed back to the road, Anna glanced in her rearview mirror and found Tatty still leaning on his hoe, watching her.

But he was no longer alone. The diminutive, bent figure of old Mrs. Baker stood beside him.

Anna stopped at the end of the drive, her eyes riveted to the mirror, watching them. Was it just her imagination, or were their expressions a little too intense?

***

Anna entered the store twenty minutes later to discover total chaos. Joss met her at the door, his hat pushed back on his head and a murderous look on his handsome face. "You just stay behind me, darlin'. If he tries to touch ya I'll knock his ass across the room and then sit on him until he freezes to death."

Anna opened her mouth to respond but didn't get the chance.

"You bitch! You're not gonna get away with this." A red-faced Mason Bethesda took a couple of steps toward her, his thick finger jabbing the air in front of him.

Pratt grabbed for the man's arm and gave it a jerk. "Take a deep breath, Mayor Bethesda. If you touch a hair on that woman's head, I'll call the cops *and* the news."

Joss nodded, crossing his arms over his broad chest. "Puke's growin' on me."

Anna rolled her eyes at her resident ghost and stepped past him. "Mr. Mayor. What exactly do you think I'm not going to get away with?"

Bethesda spared Pratt a glance, his gray eyes widening slightly as the result of Pratt's threat. But he was way too pissed off to let Pratt's threats stop him. He turned back to Anna. The deep red color that stained his lean, chiseled cheeks deepened to purple. "Don't you play coy with me, Miss Yesterday. First the phone calls and now this bullcrap. If you think you're going to extort money from me you've got another think coming!"

"Phone calls?"

Mayor Bethesda jerked his arm from Pratt's and surged forward, fists outstretched. Several things happened in quick succession.

Pratt grabbed the mayor's jacket and wrenched him backward, only to get a fairly respectable punch to the jaw for his troubles. Bethesda surged toward Anna again, rage sparking in his eyes. Before Joss could move, the air in front of Mason shimmered and Bess stuck a brightly clad, sleekly made leg out in front of the charging man, catching him on the shin. Mason grunted and his eyes went wide as he hit an obstruction he couldn't see, his arms flailing as he toppled forward. Joss met the mayor's chin with an uppercut as he fell, snapping his head back, and Bethesda hit the ground hard, with a resounding "Umph!".

Anna panicked and ran over to help him up. "Mayor Bethesda, are you all right?" She reached for his arm but he swung it sideways, hitting her hard on the thigh. Anna cried out and fell backward, but she never hit the floor. A strong pair of hands caught her and helped her stand. She turned, looking up into Pratt's handsome face and gave him a tremulous smile. Tears flooded her eyes from the pain in her leg. "Thanks, Pratt."

He gave her a curt nod, his expression murderous. "Go lock yourself in your workroom, Anna. I'm going to take out this trash and then make a couple of phone calls."

"You'll do no such thing!" The mayor exclaimed as he shoved himself off the floor. He stood, vibrating with rage, and brushed at his thousand-dollar suit. "If you do, I'll tell them how your sweet little boss lady's been trying to blackmail me over some stupid vanity newspaper."

Anna blinked. "Mayor Bethesda! Wherever did you get that idea? I simply found the paper and wanted to check into the story because it was news to me."

Bethesda snorted angrily. "And it never occurred to you that a rumor like that would just about kill my election chances?"

She frowned. "Of course it did, but that's a long way from blackmail. Why do you think I'd want to do that to you, sir?"

"Money is a powerful motivation, Miss Yesterday. Or is it something else? Are you by any chance acquainted with my opponent?"

She shook her head. "What are you implying?"

"Peter Cui is a good-looking single man. Maybe the two of you have cooked this up to ruin me."

"Sir, I…"

"Save it! I'll get to the bottom of this. And when I do, you'll be sorry you tried to destroy my career, little lady. *Very* sorry."

"Mayor Bethesda, I promise I'm not trying to do anything to you."

"Then give me that paper."

Anna blinked, his request catching her unaware. "Oh, I um…" Every instinct told her not to give him the newspaper. There was something behind the story on the yellowed newsprint and she wasn't willing to let him cover it up. "I'm sorry. I can't do that."

He held her gaze for a long moment, his hands clenched in fists at his sides and his coldly handsome face murderous.

Pratt moved up next to Anna and Joss moved in on her other side.

The mayor finally jerked his chin downward in a nod. "Then it's on, Miss Yesterday. You'll rue the day you decided to engage this battle, little lady. I promise you that."

***

As Mayor Bethesda slammed out of the store Anna sagged, suddenly overcome with the shakes. Joss grabbed her arm on one side and Pratt grabbed the other. He eyed her other, uplifted arm and Anna lowered it, flashing him a smile. "Thanks, Pratt."

"No worries, boss. You looked like you might fall down there for a minute."

"I meant for standing up for me. It means a lot."

He started to lead her toward the counter and her stool so Joss let go of her, scowling at Pratt.

"Do you have any idea what he was talking about? Blackmail? Phone calls?" Pratt shook his head. "Sounds like the plot to a really bad movie."

She laughed. "I have no idea. Somebody must be trying to extort money from him and, since I came forward with that newspaper, he thinks it's me." She sighed. "As usual my timing is impeccable."

"He can't really think you would resort to blackmail? That would be stupid. You have a business to run in Crocker." Pratt leaned an elbow on the counter and focused his sexy golden-brown gaze on her. He stood so close she could feel the warmth of his big body against her chilled skin. His scent infused the air around them, catching Anna off guard and sending spirals of unexpected lust twisting through her. She glanced quickly away, crossing her legs.

"I got the impression the mayor isn't thinking at all. He's obviously running scared." She lifted her gaze to her assistant. "There's only one reason why he'd be so scared."

Pratt nodded. "Something about that newspaper story you have is either true, or close enough to the truth not to make much difference."

She nodded, not bothering to deny the fact that she had the article. Anna looked into Pratt's eyes and, for a moment, forgot to breathe. He was so hot. So incredibly sexy. And his spirited protection of her moments earlier only solidified the knight in shining armor persona she'd been subconsciously fashioning around him. A sexy hero was hard for any woman to resist.

***

Pratt's gaze drifted downward, to her mouth, and his jaw tightened against the emotions his beautiful boss engendered in him. He swallowed hard and stepped away, unwilling to let her see the stark desire he knew drenched his gaze. He knew because he'd caught his own reflection in the mirror once when he looked at her. He'd looked like a love-sick dog.

The air behind him chilled and something moved just outside his range of sight. Pratt turned his head and saw nothing. He did an internal head shake, admonishing himself. He was starting to think he was losing his mind.

Stay away from her, puke.

Pratt jumped and flipped around.

"Pratt? Are you all right?"

When he looked at Anna she was frowning, but she appeared to be looking past him. "I…I'm fine. I just thought I heard something," he responded.

Her gaze slid to him and softened. She bit her bottom lip, looking as if she was on the verge of a decision. She glanced at her watch. "I'll tell you what…I have a couple of hours of work in the back but, when I'm done with that, how about I take you to dinner? I'd like to thank you for defending me to Bethesda."

Pratt was tempted to take her up on her offer, even if she was probably only doing it out of guilt for turning him down earlier. But he didn't believe in taking advantage of women and she'd been right when she'd told him it wasn't a good idea. He shook his head. "That's not necessary. Though I will walk you to your car tonight, if you don't mind. I don't trust that guy not to come after you again."

He almost changed his mind when her pretty face lost its smile.

"Oh, okay. I'd appreciate that. Thanks." She slid down from her stool and walked past, carefully avoiding his gaze. He watched her go, feeling like a complete jerk. Especially when his mind played auditory tricks on him again.

Nice work, no-account.

"Piss off," Pratt murmured to his imaginary friend. He was rewarded with a blast of chill air that made him shiver. He really needed to get the repair company out to check Anna's air conditioning unit. It seemed to be operating in fits and starts lately.

CHAPTER FIVE

Pierce Johnson came into the store just before closing. Pratt looked up from the money he was counting and smiled at the boy. His smile went completely unnoticed. The Johnson boy never looked him the eye. "Hi, there."

"You're not the cowboy."

Pratt blinked. "I played one once in a school play."

Pierce frowned. "That's a funny answer."

"Which explains why you're frowning," Pratt said as he came around from behind the counter. "Can I help you find something?"

"No. I found it. I came to see my bike."

Pierce stood next to a bike from the nineteen fifties whose tires were worn and metal bumpers were more rust than red paint. "You're buying that bike?"

"Not yet. I'm carefully considering my purchase. The man at the hardware said you should carefully consider every purchase. Impulse buying is wicked. At least that's what the man said. But he smells funny so I'm not sure if I can believe him." Pierce's cheeks reddened and he glanced over Pratt's shoulder. "That was inappropriate. I'm being inappropriate."

The comment and its delivery sounded so much like a mother's scolding that Pratt had to smile. He covered his mouth with his hand, clearing his throat so Pierce wouldn't know. "You can fix that right up and it will be a really nice bike."

"That's what the cowboy said." He looked around the store. "I need to talk to the cowboy, where is he?"

Pratt's mouth opened but he didn't know what to say. He knew the boy was autistic. Anna had told him about the Johnsons on his first day so he'd know how to handle Pierce. But he didn't think delusions were part of autism. "Did you meet the cowboy here?"

Pierce reached toward the bike's cracked, vinyl banana seat, his fingers skimming the air just above it before returning to pluck at his shirt. "You're not very observant, are you?"

Pratt rolled his lips. "I take it the cowboy's here a lot."

"He guards the store. I'm surprised you don't know that since you work here." Pierce looked up and, just for a beat, his dark blue gaze met Pratt's. "Or are you just here to get into Miss Anna's pants?" Pierce frowned. "That's what my mother said. But that was inappropriate. Even I know that." He shook his head. "She didn't know I was listening. But I was."

"Obviously," Pratt murmured. He was surprisingly bothered by the Johnson woman's comment. "This is my job. I think Miss Anna is very nice. I hope she and I will be good friends. But I have no intention of getting in her pants."

Pierce's non-touch skimmed above the back fender, halting over a small dent. "That's good. You'd look really bad in her pants. You'd probably split the seams."

Pratt's snort of laughter brought Pierce's head up. The boy smiled. "That was a joke. I made a funny joke."

Pratt nodded and opened his mouth to agree that the joke was funny, but Pierce was no longer paying attention to Pratt, he was looking at something to Pratt's right.

"Hi, hoss."

***

41

Joss tipped his hat back and smiled. "You're hoss."

Pierce laughed. "No, you are."

"Come to buy that bike, finally?"

"I'm considering. I won't be bullied into making a purchase just because you're a cowboy."

The puke looked from the boy to the spot of empty air next to him and frowned. "What's your friend's name, Pierce?"

Joss grinned, crossing his arms over his chest. "Tell him my name is Harvey."

Pierce snorted. "Jimmy Stewart! I saw that movie, it was very entertaining."

"Your friend's name is Jimmy Stewart?"

"No." Pierce glared at Pratt. "It's Harvey."

Pratt frowned, then seemed to think a change of subject was in order. "About that bike. I could fix it up for you."

"No. I want to fix it up myself."

"Oh, do you know how?"

Pierce's hand stopped plucking at his shirt and he turned an angry look on Pratt. His dark eyebrows were lowered over downcast eyes and his jaw was clenched. "It's my bike. If you touch it then it won't be mine!"

Joss decided he'd better step in before the puke created a real fix. "Listen here, boy, the guy's a coot but Miss Anna trusts him to mend things. I guess you can trust him to help you with that bike anyways."

Pierce's jaw lost some of its tension and he seemed to calm. His glance swung back to the bike. "Will you help too, hoss?"

Recognizing the signs of capitulation, Joss grinned. "I will, but if you keep callin' me hoss you'll have to get a new name 'cause that's your name."

The boy laughed, shaking his head. "I'm hoss one. You can be hoss two."

"I'm older. I reckon I should be hoss one." Joss leaned against a hundred-year-old hutch and it creaked.

The puke's gaze flew toward the hutch.

"You didn't want to be any hoss before. Now you're just being difficult." Pierce dropped his fingers to the bike, finally touching it. Joss recognized the look on the boy's face. He was laying claim to the battered toy.

Joss laughed. "Okay, you win. You're number one."

The puke stepped forward, reaching for the bike. Pierce's face darkened and his eyes widened in horror. "No!"

Joss whipped an arm out and smacked it against Pratt's hand, knocking it away from the bike. The puke stopped dead in his tracks and turned, his eyes staring right into Joss's without seeing him.

The puke stepped back, rubbing his arm, just as Anna emerged from the back room. Joss turned to her. "This here kid wants to buy the bike, darlin'. But he don't want nobody else touchin' it. You need to let the boy haul it to the back room himself so the puke can tell him how to mend it."

***

Anna blinked, her gaze sliding worriedly to Pratt. But she didn't dare do more than glare at Joss with Pratt there. "Hello, Pierce." She offered Pratt a smile. "Pierce doesn't like anyone touching his things." She lifted her eyebrows, praying he'd get the message. She was relieved when he nodded.

"Of course. I told him I'd help him fix it up. Mind if we use the workroom?"

"Absolutely. I think we have most of what you'll need there. We can recover that seat, paint the frame, and I think I even have some spare reflectors back there."

Pierce glanced up. "Where's the cowboy? I need to tell him about the man at the hardware."

"He had to go somewhere, Pierce." Anna widened her eyes at Pratt, telling him without words to just go along. "When he comes back, I'll tell him you need to talk to him."

Pierce nodded, plucking at his shirt. "Miss Yesterday, that's good. The cowboy guards the store. He needs to know about the man at the hardware. I need to tell him."

She nodded, avoiding Pratt's gaze. "He does, yes. It's very smart of you to know that Pierce."

"I'm not stupid, Miss Yesterday." The boy's tone was so disgusted it was all Anna could do not to laugh. But she couldn't help sharing a smile with Pratt.

***

Anna pulled the door to the store closed and locked it. "Thanks for walking me to my car, Pratt. I'm sure it's not necessary…"

"It's necessary, if nothing else so I don't worry. That Bethesda guy is certifiable."

She dropped her keys into her purse and started walking alongside him. It was just after six o'clock in the evening and, as usual, the streets were quiet, everyone having gone home for dinner and the evening's activities. Only Pete's Diner was still open a few blocks down. It was one of the things Anna loved most and liked least about living in a small town. Work and home were balanced evenly, which meant that not much got accomplished after five o'clock. But it also meant life was richer, filled with love, friends, and family. And the pace was slower.

High overhead the sky was darkening for the rain she could smell building. In the distance a low roll of thunder announced the coming storm. The oppressive heat of the day had been swept away on a soft, ozone-filled breeze, making it a pleasant night for a walk.

"Gonna rain."

She lifted her face to the sky and inhaled deeply, enjoying the scent of the storm. "It is." She smiled.

"You like the rain?"

"I love storms. Something about them brings out the romance in my soul."

He nodded, touching the small of her back to nudge her farther from the curb as a car headed too fast down the street. Anna felt that slight touch all the way to her toes. Her body heated and purred under it. She looked down, rubbing the gooseflesh that had risen on her arms.

A small red car flashed by, wafting them with quickly cooling air.

"Here." Pratt took off the denim shirt he'd worn over his usual tee shirt and settled it over her shoulders. "You should have worn a sweater."

She laughed. "It was ninety degrees when I left home this morning. I think it's dropped twenty degrees." The shirt was deliciously warm and smelled of him. She inhaled surreptitiously.

"That means the storm's gonna be a good one."

They stepped into the small gravel parking lot at the center of town. "I'm glad you're keeping me company, Pratt. I'll admit I was a little spooked after Mason's visit. I've never seen him like that. He was totally unhinged."

Pratt leaned on the car, crossing strong arms over his chest. The street lights blinked on in the early dark and their soft glow illuminated the hair on his head and arms, turning it to burnished gold. "It was my pleasure. And don't worry, we'll get to the bottom of the Bethesda problem. I'm kind of good at that sort of thing."

She dug her keys out of her purse but made no move to unlock her car. Instead, she leaned against it and looked up at him. "Your resume said you'd been a cop. Why did you leave your job and come to Indiana?"

He glanced away, clearly reluctant to answer her question. "Let's just say I wasn't cut out to be a cop."

She waited but, when he didn't elaborate, she unlocked the car door. "Well…I'm glad you're here. It's nice having a man around. Just in case."

He reached out and touched her hand as she pulled the door handle. "I'm glad too, Anna. You have a good night now."

He leaned close, his head lowering slightly and Anna held her breath. She thought he was going to kiss her. She should stop him. She knew she should. But instead she swallowed and found herself leaning closer. His heat enveloped her, chasing away the chilled air and cocooning her in his delicious scent. Anna's lips parted as his head lowered, his hands gently framing her arms to pull her close. Her eyes closed. She tilted toward him. His lips touched her cheek, lingered softly, and then lifted away.

" 'Night, Anna."

She opened her eyes and watched him walk away, surprised to discover she was disappointed. Worse than disappointed really. She was bereft at the loss of his heat and touch.

Lightning slashed across the sky, bathing him in silver light, and thunder followed quickly. The first fat drops of rain pinged against the car and Anna shook herself out of the haze Pratt's touch had caused, sliding quickly behind the wheel.

A heartbeat later, rain dropped out of the sky in sheets so thick she couldn't see much beyond her windshield. She hoped Pratt had been able to duck inside the diner before it hit.

CHAPTER SIX

Anna pulled her tea out of the microwave, shivering as she blew on it. She'd gotten soaked running from her car to her second-floor apartment over the carpet store slash funeral parlor on the West edge of town.

She'd changed into sweats and toweled her hair but it was still damp and, though she'd turned off the air conditioner and started a fire in the gas fireplace, she still felt chilled. Settling on the couch, she tucked her feet under her and flipped on the television set. The fifty-inch flat screen hanging over her fireplace was her sole indulgence in the cozy but simple apartment. She'd rationalized the expense by telling herself she often did the books in front of the TV at night, so it really was kind of a business expense. If she really stretched the boundaries of the concept.

Anna set her tea on the coffee table and reached for her battered, leather briefcase. Pulling it onto her lap, she dug around looking for the bills she'd intended to pay while she watched a DVRed episode of a popular vampire series.

She found her ledger, but the bills were missing. "Dangit!" She'd been so discombobulated by the excitement at the store she'd forgotten to grab them before she left. She sat back, her finger on the play button of her remote. The last thing she wanted to do was go back out into the rain to retrieve the bills. Unfortunately, a couple of them were past due and she'd hoped to get them into the mail the next morning so the utilities at the store didn't get shut off.

It was unlike her to be so scattered. She'd always prided herself in keeping on top of things like bills. Dropping her head to the back of the couch, Anna swore softly. She would have to go back to the store. If she didn't, she'd stress about it all night anyway.

Sighing, she took a last sip of tea and slipped her feet into her flip flops, scuffing her way to the door. It would only take a few minutes to drive to the store and grab the bundle of bills. And then she'd be able to relax and enjoy the rest of her evening.

Grabbing her purse, Anna headed outside, dismayed to discover that the rain was still coming down hard. Oversized drops pinged against the awning over her stairs as she descended quickly toward street level. A wide, glistening puddle dominated the sidewalk at the bottom of the stairs. Anna pulled her sweats up and stepped into it, sucking in a breath as cold water rose to her ankles.

The rain she'd enjoyed earlier was really starting to lose some of its magic. She ran to her car, stepping into an unseen puddle a few feet from the sidewalk and splashing muddy water up her leg. Swearing like a sailor, Anna pressed the unlock button on her key fob and wrenched the car door open, diving inside.

Five minutes later she parked at the yellow curb in front of her store. At that point she didn't even care if she got a ticket. She was just going to be inside for a minute anyway. She unlocked and opened the door, reaching toward the alarm pad. The green light glowed through the dark.

Apparently, she'd forgotten to set it when she left. Closing her eyes, Anna banged her forehead against the door frame a couple of times, thoroughly disgusted with herself. Heading through the store toward her workshop door, she prayed that one of her spectral friends didn't pay her a visit. She just wanted to get in and get out, fast.

Her workroom door was open, causing her to frown. She always made it a habit to keep the door closed so customers couldn't see the chaos beyond the door. She must have been in a total daze when she left earlier that night.

But as soon as she stepped through the door, she knew something was wrong. The floor crunched under her flip flop as she stepped down. It sounded like broken glass. She turned, reaching for the light switch. Suddenly the night moved and something large and dark rushed her. It hit her shoulder with the force of a charging bull and pain radiated down her arm. Anna cried out and flew backward, her head hitting the wall. She saw stars, her vision swimming, and heard the sound of footsteps pounding toward the front door.

Pain jolted through her skull and she reached up, touching the back of her head, where a bump was already starting to form. She sat there for a minute, listening, but there were no other sounds in the store. She planted a hand and started to shove herself off the floor. Sharp pain sluiced through her palm as she pressed her hand into a shard of glass.

"Ouch, darn it!" She jerked her hand back, tears sliding down her face. "Joss!"

Where the heck was he?

A cool breeze wafted over her, filled with the scent of rain. The sound of water hitting the ground was too clear. She looked to her left and saw that the window in the back door had been broken out.

"He's gone." Bess's usually snotty tone sounded positively terrified. "That miserable varmint took him." Her words ended on a sob and Anna panicked. Bess never cried. Anna had known the ghost for almost five years and, during that time, nothing had even made her heavily painted lip quiver.

Anna forgot the pain in her head and hand. "Gone? How can he be gone?" But even as she said the words Anna knew. With a panicked cry she shoved herself off the ground and ran toward her office. She flipped the light switch and stared in horror at the mess that had been made in the cozy space. The desk drawers hung at odd angles from their tracks. A couple of them were obviously broken from the rough treatment. The desktop was clear, all of the folders and paperwork she'd had on its surface flung about the room. Her file cabinets had been toppled onto their dented sides, the drawers open and folders flung around. The pictures from the walls had been thrown to the ground, their glass scattered over the carpet and nestled like little daggers among the papers. Even her potted palm had been upended, the rich, black dirt staining everything within a three-foot radius of its pot. Anna barely registered any of that. Her gaze slid to the heavy metal object nestled against the far wall.

The door on her little safe was hanging open, its contents spilling out onto the floor. She dropped to her knees with a little cry, rifling quickly through the items in the safe. It was mostly paperwork she didn't want to lose or get destroyed. Everything appeared to be there. All except for Joss's gun belt. It was gone.

Anna pushed to her feet, terror sliding through to twist her stomach. "Joss," she whispered.

"We have to get him back."

Anna turned a dazed look toward the ceiling, where Bess hovered in an insubstantial form. The mouthy specter was too upset even to completely manifest. Her horrendous clown makeup ran in bright rivulets down her pale cheeks as she cried. "We just have to." She succumbed to full-out sobs, her hysteria causing the overhead light to blink erratically and the papers in the room to take flight.

"Bess, did you see the guy who took Joss's gun belt? What did he look like?"

The sobbing specter shook her head, sniffling loudly. "He had somethin' over his head."

In a horrified daze, Anna dropped her butt into her office chair and stared into space, trying to think. Who would take Joss's gun belt and why? Nobody even knew about it or its importance to her.

Except for her friend Denise. Anna replayed her friend's visit to the shop the day before and frowned. She shook her head. Denise would never trash her office or steal something important from her. Why would she?

Anyone who saw the gun belt in the safe would know it was valuable. In a store full of items that had value, she only kept a few things in that safe. It would be pretty clear to anyone who saw it there that the belt was important...in some way...to her.

She dropped her head into her hands and tried to block out the sound of Bess's shrieking. She had to do something. But what? Her head came up, a thought occurred that had her hand reaching for her phone. Before she could consider what she was about to do, she was dialing Pratt's number. It was time to call in the one person with police experience whom she could trust with a really big secret.

Hopefully, he wouldn't think she'd lost her mind.

***

Pratt just stood there, staring at the woman he'd had some really inappropriate fantasies about, wondering if she'd lost her mind. His ears heard what she said but his mind just didn't want to go there. Sure, he knew better than most that paranormal events occurred. He'd even been mixed up in a few of those "events" himself. But if there had been a ghost in the store, he would have known it.

Wouldn't he?

Then he thought about all the times he'd felt the touch of something he couldn't see. All the times a wash of chill air had swept over him. He remembered his imaginary friend. And the Pierce Johnson thing... "Is this the cowboy?"

Some of the panic eased from Anna's pretty face and she smiled. "Yes. That's Joss."

"So, the boy, Pierce, can see him?"

She frowned slightly. "Apparently, though that surprises me."

"You can see him."

"Yes."

"Who else can see him?"

"Nobody. At least not that I know of."

He stared at her another minute, until he realized she'd begun to squirm again. Then he forced himself to look away.

"I know it sounds crazy…" Her voice trailed off and she twined her fingers nervously together in her lap.

Pratt wished he could make it easier for her, but… "A ghost from the eighteen hundreds?"

She took a deep breath and nodded.

"And he's tied to the store through this gun belt?"

The overhead light started flickering again and Pratt looked up, frowning. "What's wrong with that light?"

Anna shrugged, glancing upward. "That's Bess. She's a little upset. She and Joss are very…close."

"Bess?" Pratt cleared his throat, embarrassed by the schoolboy squeak in his voice. "Don't tell me you have another ghost?"

"Okay, I won't tell you." Anna's lips tightened to hide a smile.

Pratt swore softly. He thought about it for a minute and then crossed his arms over his chest. "Where is she?"

Anna pointed toward the ceiling, in the back corner. Pratt stared at the spot but saw nothing. He walked over and stood beneath the spot she'd indicated. The air was definitely chillier there. But he still saw nothing. "Bess, if you can hear me, make the light flicker twice."

"She doesn't do that kind of th…" The light flickered two times and Anna's voice trailed off.

Pratt nodded. "Bess, don't you worry. We're gonna get Joss back. Okay?"

The light flickered again and Pratt turned back to Anna. "I don't like the timing of this thing. First you find that newspaper, then Bethesda shows up screaming like an ass, and then your place gets broken into."

Anna's face was incredulous. "You think Mason Bethesda had something to do with this?"

"I'd say it's almost a certainty. I don't believe in coincidences. Did the thief get the newsprint?"

Her eyes widened. "Oh. I don't know. Something told me it wasn't secure in the safe so I hid it." She frowned, wishing she'd had the same thought for Joss's gun belt.

"Can you check please?"

Anna chewed her bottom lip, obviously reluctant to let him see where she'd hidden it.

Irritation flitted through him but, even so, he understood her reluctance. "I can go wait in the workroom."

"No." Anna sighed. "I need to trust somebody." She stood up and walked over to the corner of her office where Bess hovered, stepping up onto an old wooden dining room chair. She reached her arms over her head and shoved a water-stained ceiling tile up, reaching into the opening with her other hand. A look of relief softened her features. "It's still here."

Pratt stood near while she replaced the newspaper and the ceiling tile, his hands up to catch her if she wobbled. "That's good at least. We still have some leverage. But I'm afraid that's why they took the gun belt."

Anna stepped carefully from the chair, braced by Pratt's grip, and stood with her fingers still clasped in his. Her soft hands were icy cold. Before he thought about what he was doing, Pratt had started to rub them between his own hands to warm them.

She blinked in surprise but didn't try to retrieve her hands. "I don't understand. There's no possible way anybody could have known about Joss and the gun belt." But she frowned slightly and bit her lip.

"What, Anna? What aren't you telling me?"

She sighed. "I did tell one person about the article. And she saw the gun belt in my safe."

"Who?"

"My friend, Denise. But she would never do this to me."

"You'd be surprised what people will do," he told her. "When did you show her the article?"

"Earlier today."

"Does she have any connection to Bethesda?"

Anna's gaze slipped away.

"Anna? I can't help you if you aren't going to be honest with me."

"She used to date Mason. A few years ago. But she hates him now."

"Maybe. Or maybe not. Sometimes people tell us what they think we want to hear." He reached out and touched her face. "We need to consider that she might be involved in this."

Anna frowned but nodded.

Thinking about what she'd told him, Pratt lifted her hands to chest height and rubbed more briskly. Her eyes widened and she licked her lips. He didn't know if she was warming from his ministrations but he certainly was. "But they knew it must be valuable because of where you had it. They're probably hoping it's important enough to you that you'll give up the paper for it."

She nodded, her gaze growing soft as her hands finally warmed under his touch. Pratt stopped rubbing but found it very difficult to release her hands. "Is it?"

She blinked, her eyes refocusing. "What?"

"Is the gun belt important enough for you to give up the paper?" Pratt heard the edge in his voice as he asked the question and realized that what he was really asking her was if Joss was important to her. When her pretty eyes filled with tears, he had his answer.

He didn't like it much.

"I'd give anything to get him back, Pratt." Her voice broke on the words and tears slipped down her cheeks. He resisted the urge to reach out and swipe the glistening drops from her face. "Then we'll make a trade. It's going to be all right, Anna. I promise."

She sniffled, nodding. "Okay, what do we do first?"

"We wait for the thief to contact us."

Her shoulders drooped and she looked so despondent he relented. "But we might as well try to figure out what's going on while we wait. If we can figure out the story behind the newsprint, we might not even need the paper."

She straightened, swiping the tears from her face. "Good. If Bethesda is behind this, I'm gonna get the bastard."

Pratt smiled, finally giving in to his urge to touch her cheek. "That's my girl." When she smiled, Pratt realized he was in trouble. Big trouble. He was losing his heart fast, and he would do anything at that moment to keep the tears from ever returning to Anna's beautiful face. Even if it meant rescuing his arch-rival for her affections. A cowboy. And a damn ghost.

Flippin' wonderful.

CHAPTER SEVEN

Where in tarnation was he? Joss had experienced a horrendous ripping sensation and had lost awareness for a time. When he'd come back to himself, he'd been in a strange, dirty little room. Joss looked around the unfamiliar place, thinking it wasn't fit for a mangy dog, let alone a ghost who was used to a clean, airy store filled with comforting items from the past.

Dented metal and cardboard that was shaped like furniture didn't comfort him. He drifted toward the ceiling and tried to peer out of the single, dingy window. All he saw were feet. Feet and ankles. A familiar flash of yellow went by on the street and Joss frowned. The artistic boy who didn't like to be touched had a two-wheeled vehicle that color. Hope filled Joss's breast. Maybe he was mistaken. Could he be in a basement room of the antique store where he'd never been before?

He tried again to leave the room but he hit the wall as if he were made of flesh and blood. "Dangit" He pounded on the door. "Let me out of here, you rascals!"

Nobody came. Nobody seemed to hear. He settled down in the room's only chair, frowning. The ratty chair smelled musty and had mouse droppings on it. Joss set his mind to considerin'. There had to be a way to get back to Anna and Yesterday's Antiques. All he had to do was put his mind to it and he'd find a way out of the fix he found himself in.

Then vamoose as fast as he could.

***

"You sure there's a house back here?"

Anna grinned at Pratt. "I've been here before. Several times."

Pratt pulled his Jeep Cherokee down the Baker's driveway and slowed when he saw a shiny white truck parked behind Tatty's more elderly pickup. "Looks like they already have company."

Anna straightened, peering through the windshield at the long, front porch, where two rocking chairs were currently being put through their paces. "Good. There's old Mrs. Baker."

"Who's that she's talking to?"

"Looks like… Huh, that's old Mr. Gilfer. He owns the hardware store in downtown Crocker."

Pratt pulled up behind the big, white truck and turned the key, murmuring to Anna. "He looks like he's about a hundred."

She smiled. "Close, I think he's in his late eighties."

"Much better." Pratt laughed, shaking his head.

Anna climbed out of the jeep and walked toward the porch, lifting her hand in a wave. "Hello, Mrs. Baker, Mr. Gilfer. How are you today?"

The wizened old woman sitting in the first rocker pursed her lips and squinted. "That you, Anna girl?"

Anna climbed the two steps to the porch and clasped one of the woman's soft hands between her own. "It is. You're looking wonderful, ma'am."

The woman's lips twisted and she laughed. "Go on now. I got prunes in my kitchen with smoother skin on 'em than I got." She lifted her gaze as Pratt walked up. "My, my. Who is this tall fella?"

"This is my assistant, Pratt. Pratt, this is Mrs. Baker. She has the best-canned peaches in the state."

The old woman lifted her hand like the Queen of England and grinned widely as Pratt bent over it, kissing its walnut colored surface. "Nice to meet you, ma'am."

She tittered like a young virgin.

"What business you youngsters have out here?"

Anna turned to the elderly man scowling in the next chair. "We just need to ask Mrs. Baker a few questions. You don't mind if we steal her for a few minutes, do you?"

"'Pears I do." The old man lowered bushy white eyebrows and fixed a suspicious glare on Pratt. "I don't even know this young man."

Pratt decided that Anna must have a deep well of patience. She looked serene as she introduced them. "Mr. Gilfer, this is Pratt. He works with me at my store."

"Yesterday's Antiques?"

She smiled. "That's the place. Remember, you sold me that beautiful dining room set last year?"

The eyebrows lowered even farther, essentially obscuring the beady, brown eyes beneath them. "That set belonged to my mother."

"It did. I remember. Such a beautiful set. I promise you I asked a fortune for it and the young woman who bought it was happy to pay it."

He inclined his chin in a brisk nod. "Good. She *should* pay a lot. That set belonged to my mother."

Anna bit her bottom lip and nudged Pratt as he expelled an impatient breath. "In fact, I was wondering if you had any more items you'd like to sell. Your mother's wonderful things are always in demand. She took such good care of them." Anna pulled up a chair on the other side of Mr. Gilfer and drew his attention away from Pratt and Mrs. Baker. Taking her cue, Pratt did the same, sitting down on the porch swing at the other end of the porch. He started off by asking Mrs. Baker about her peaches. Then they got into a spirited discussion about her peach jelly and worked their way up to her tomatoes and the wonderful things she could make with them. Pratt found himself asking to buy several things before he even realized it. The old woman appeared fragile and slightly off-kilter. But his instincts told him she was sharp as a tack. And she played her mark better than any of the con men he'd encountered as a cop. He'd be lucky to leave the Baker place without several hundred dollars' worth of foodstuffs in the back of his car.

To save his wallet he deftly changed the subject. "I understand you sold that beautiful dresser to Anna."

The old woman nodded, looking sad. "That ol' dresser was in my family for decades."

Pratt nodded, barely resisting the urge to ask her why she'd sold it. That was not only a very personal question, but Anna wouldn't thank him for making her clients second guess selling her their antiques. "It's interesting, when we were repairing that bottom drawer…"

"I ain't givin' you the money back, son. I tol' the girl that drawer was a bit stickish."

Pratt lifted his hands. "I don't want any money back, ma'am. We fixed the drawer. It's fine. But we found something inside the drawer."

She scratched her chin and her faded, brown gaze slipped away, focusing on a cardinal pecking at the grass beyond the porch. "Such pretty birds. I al'ays liked them cardinals."

Pratt didn't fall for her act. He saw the sharpness behind the feigned blank gaze. "It was a page from a newspaper, dated July 12th, 1964. Do you remember that date? Any idea where you might have gotten the newspaper, ma'am?"

Her gnarled fingers plucked the arms of the rocker. She turned to him, her gaze slightly hostile, but it didn't quite meet his. "Now why would you ask me that question?"

"The newsprint has a story on it we're curious about, that's all. Anna and I are trying to find out more about it."

She smiled, scratching her nose. "I could'a picked it up anywhere, son. I don't like to waste stuff."

"It was singed around the edges."

Her head snapped around and her lips parted, shock clear in her expression. She didn't speak for a moment but then she frowned. "I remember now. Old Mr. Baker tried to burn the paper once and I grabbed it out of the fire before it caught hold. Damn wasteful was that old man. He didn't see the value in reusing things. He liked his stuff all shiny and new." She shook her head, obviously disgusted by her deceased husband's love of nice things. "Now they call it recyclin'. I been recyclin' since I was new married." She grinned at Pratt. "I'm guessin' that makes me a recyclin' pioneer."

He returned her smile. "You definitely are that. You don't remember where the paper came from?"

Shaking her head, she tugged on her long, cotton skirt. "From town, I'd guess. Where else do a paper come from?"

"Your family got the newspaper regularly?"

" 'Course! Ever'body takes the paper, don't they? I liked to read the stories every night afore bed." She nodded.

"Okay, thanks so much, Mrs. Baker." Pratt stood.

She looked up, finding his gaze. Any confusion she might have felt was apparently gone. "You're welcome, son. You just walk on around the house and see Tatty now. He'll get your things for you. You'll have to pay him in cash though. We don't take none of that plastic or paper stuff meant to replace real money. We only take the real kind, backed up by good old gov'ment gold."

Pratt didn't have the heart to tell her that "real" money hadn't been backed up by gold for quite a while. He'd let her finish out her long, long life with at least one, comforting delusion.

***

Forty minutes later Pratt's jeep was full of his and Anna's purchases and they were headed back to town. "She lied to me."

Anna frowned. "About what?"

"She said they took the newspaper."

"Tatty said they didn't."

"Right. One of them is lying."

"Not necessarily, Mrs. Baker sometimes loses herself in a fog. She's had a series of small strokes."

Pratt snorted. "If that woman is feeble-minded, my name is Cleopatra."

Anna's lips turned up in a smile. "Okay, Cleopatra. Why are you so sure she's lying?"

"Because I've studied liars for years and there are certain things to look for. Body language and speech tics."

"Such as?"

"Such as a liar won't hold your gaze. His responses are slightly off-kilter, response times are off. Liars get defensive, and evasive. When I asked her directly about the newsprint, she tried to distract me. I've handled a lot of con men over the years and that woman could work Monte Carlo as a grifter and make a fortune."

Anna sat in silence the rest of the trip. When Pratt glanced her way, she looked sad. He felt bad bursting her bubble about the old woman. But it was only going to get worse. Chances were that the person responsible for her missing gun belt was somebody she'd known all her life. Finally though, he couldn't take the silence any longer. "Do you mind if we stop at the hardware store? I need some things for the store."

Anna nodded in a distracted way but stayed immersed in her thoughts for the rest of the drive.

CHAPTER EIGHT

"You think she's the one?"

Mason Bethesda glanced at his campaign manager as he poured brandy into his coffee. "It has to be her. What are the chances that two different people would suddenly find this stupid story and start trying to blackmail me with it?"

"In fairness, the girl hasn't threatened you."

"Yet." Mason dropped into his chair and sipped from his mug. He closed his eyes as the hot liquid burned its way down his throat. "Can we sue her to get it back?"

"Only if you want the whole thing splashed across the news."

Mason swore, taking another bracing sip. "Then we have to get nasty."

His manager frowned. "What exactly do you mean by that?"

Mason fixed the younger man with an uncompromising look. "I don't know, Reese. What *do* I mean by that?"

"I'm not comfortable…"

"Would you be more comfortable getting unemployment?"

Perry Reese blanched, shifted in his chair, and then shook his head. "I'm not going to hurt her."

"I would never suggest you hurt anyone." The look he gave his campaign manager was clear. He would never suggest it…but he'd certainly expect it to be done if it was necessary.

Reese tugged the crease on his suit pants. "I guess we could threaten the store. At the very least we can send the IRS in to harass her."

"That's why I hired you, Reese. You have a very creative mind." He sipped again. "That's a fine place to start. But we need to be ready to escalate if she doesn't give that newspaper up."

"What exactly does this article say, Mason?"

Mason glared across the desk. "It doesn't matter since it's all lies."

"If it threatens the campaign I need to know. I can't fight what I can't see, Mason."

"It has nothing to do with me, if that's what you're wondering. It was my father's mess and he thought he had it covered up. But apparently something fell through the cracks." He frowned. "The girl isn't the only problem. There are three other people in town who know. They were well compensated at the time, so they've kept their mouths shut. But if this thing gets stirred back up…" He shook his head. "I might need you to expand your creative handling a bit."

Reese didn't look happy. "That many people knowing will make this difficult if not impossible to keep the lid on."

"Now Reese, you know how I feel about negativity."

"Could one of those people be blackmailing you?"

"Doubtful. They were complicit in the cover-up half a century ago. Even if they managed to take me down they'd know I wouldn't hesitate to drag them down with me."

Reese stood up and started toward the door. He stopped with his hand on the doorknob and looked back. "Mason, if this was your father's scandal, they why are you so worried about it?"

"Because it was…unpleasant. And people in this town loved my father. They thought he was a god. If they find out their god had horns, they might start wondering if *I'm* as great as they think I am. I can't afford to lose even a small percentage of votes to this thing. The race is too tight."

***

Pratt and Anna entered the front door and were greeted by the jangle of a bell and the slightly off-putting scent of chemical fertilizer. Though not a pleasant smell, Anna liked it because it brought back memories from her childhood. She and her brother used to bring their weekly allowance to the store and buy candy with it.

Gilfer's Hardware had the largest selection of candy of any store in town. Except of course for the new fudge shop on Jackson Street. Dubbed by Crocker's townies as New Crocker, the area one street over from Main was getting a second wind with eclectic shops and bars that stretched alongside the river. Based on the same concept as the Broad Ripple area in Indianapolis, Jackson Street was Crocker's attempt to pull tourists into the tiny town. It had been more successful even than they'd hoped. The only negative was that it drew a lot of strangers into town and they'd had to double their police force to handle the resulting trouble. In addition to the Town Marshal, Crocker now had four police officers instead of two and several reserve officers.

Like most of Crocker's long-timers, Anna preferred old Crocker. It was the Crocker of her youth. Heading toward the candy aisle out of habit, Anna stopped, turned to Pratt, and grinned guiltily.

"I'll take a candy bar," he told her with an answering smile.

"My choice?"

"Anything but raisins."

Pratt headed down the center aisle, looking for masking tape and spray paint for Pierce's bike project, and Anna fixed her attention on the candy.

A moment later she was pulled from a very important decision about whether to get straight chocolate or chocolate with nuts in it, by the sound of harsh whispering nearby. Something about the urgency of the whispers drew her to a nearby display of deer hunting supplies. From the sound of it, the whisperers were just on the other side of the bright orange caps and camouflage jumpsuits. Anna reached for a hat and dropped it on her head, trying to peek through the display surreptitiously.

"Where do you think it is?"

"I don't know, but I can tell you it wasn't there."

"How the hell did this happen, Beck?"

"Somebody must have told her. It wasn't me."

"Love the hat."

Anna jumped and turned to glare at Pratt. But it was too late, the harsh whispering had stopped and the sound of footsteps hurrying away was all she had left. She took a chance and walked around the display but all she saw was the tail of an orange apron disappearing through the back door. "Dammit!"

Pratt had followed her around the display and stood holding his tape and paint, a confused look on his face. "What's the matter?"

She grabbed his arm, putting her finger in front of her lips and dragging him toward the door. Pratt barely had time to yank the hunting cap off Anna's head and set his items on the counter before she pulled him out the door. The cashier, whose name was Becky according to her crooked name tag, glanced up from her fashion magazine and popped her gum in confusion. "I'll be right back," he told her. She just shrugged and went back to her article about belly-baring tees and boyfriend jeans, hip hop music blaring from her headphones.

He tugged his arm back as soon as they cleared the door. "Are you going to tell me what's going on?"

Anna looked around. "I think somebody in there was discussing the break-in at my store."

"You heard them talking about it?"

"I'm not sure. It sounded like that's what they were discussing."

He frowned. "Tell me exactly what they said."

After she related the conversation as best she could remember it, Pratt stood for a moment, looking thoughtful. "And you think one of them works in the store?"

"I saw an apron disappearing into the backroom when I came around the display."

"It could have just been bad timing. There's nothing to point directly to an employee."

Anna crossed her arms and scowled at him. "There's nothing to prove it isn't an employee either."

He held up a hand. "All right, calm down. I'm not saying I won't check into it. I just want you to be realistic."

She shoved his arm. "Whatever. Get in there and check. We might lose them while we're out here jabbering."

"*You* dragged *me* out here, remember?"

She flipped a dismissive hand at him. "Go on. I'll watch the front door and talk to anyone who comes out, see if I can recognize the voice."

Pratt shook his head. "You're very bossy, Miss Anna."

"Shoo."

"I'm going. Do you know who Beck might be?"

"Not a clue. The owner's son pretty much runs the place now and his name's Frank. Old Mr. Gilfer is semi-retired."

"Could you have heard Beck and they said Frank?"

Anna thought about it. "It's possible, I guess. They were whispering. But I'm pretty sure I heard Beck."

***

Pratt left her outside to guard the front, his lips turning up in a smile at the idea of his diminutive boss protecting anything. If he thought she was in real danger he would have made her come with him. But it was probably better if she stayed outside. She was too emotional and he needed to proceed with caution.

He approached the preoccupied cashier and waited for her to lower her magazine and look at him. She reached for his items without removing her earbuds. Pratt placed his hand on the tape to stop her, miming for her to lift the headphones.

She dragged them backward, letting them rest on the back of her neck, and gave him a put-upon look as only a teenager can do.

"Thanks," he told her with a smile. "I was wondering if I could talk to Beck."

She stared at him for a minute and popped her gum. The words finally seemed to penetrate the fog of her mind and she shook her head. "There is no Beck. I'm Becky, but I don't even know you. Aside from me, we have a Frank and a Susan. You want to talk to one of them?"

"Sure. I'll talk to Frank." Pratt enhanced the voltage on his smile and was rewarded with an agitated sigh. Obviously summoning Frank was an even greater hardship than taking a break from her music had been. Becky picked up a microphone and pressed a button, summoning Frank from the depths of the store in a bored monotone.

"I appreciate it," Pratt told her. "I'll just go meet him." She shrugged and tugged her headphones back up to her ears, already dismissing him.

Pratt headed for the door at the back of the store, expecting to see Frank emerging wearing an orange apron.

"Can I help you?"

Pratt jerked to a stop halfway through the store and turned. A man who looked to be about sixty approached him with a smile. "I'm looking for Frank."

The man extended a hand. "You found him. I'm Frank Gilfer. How can I help you?"

Frank Gilfer had thinning gray hair and black eyebrows over small, brown eyes. He wasn't wearing the store's signature orange apron. Instead, he had on a navy-blue polo with "Gilfer's Hardware" embroidered on the pocket and light-colored khakis. Pratt shook the man's hand, noting the calluses that bespoke a lifetime of honest labor. "I'm Pratt Davies. I work at Yesterday's Antiques."

Frank nodded. "Yes. I think I've seen you there. You're new."

"I am. I'm also new in town. Anna was kind enough to give me an opportunity."

"That sounds like her. She's a really great kid. How are things going over there?"

Pratt frowned, stuffing his hands in his pockets. "Not so good, actually. She had a break-in last night."

Frank's eyebrows lifted in surprise. "Oh, I'm sorry to hear that. Did she lose anything valuable?"

"Only her sense of safety." Pratt watched the store manager carefully. He did seem a bit nervous. "That's why I'm here, actually. The window in the back door was broken. I wondered if I could bring the door in and have you replace the glass this afternoon?"

Frank nodded, clapping Pratt on the shoulder. "Absolutely. I'll make sure it gets done quickly."

"Good. Thanks. You don't happen to know a locksmith too? Under the circumstances, I think it would be a good idea to change all the locks."

Frank pulled a business card from his khaki slacks and wrote a number on the back. "Try Handi-Locks, out on the south side of town. They're quick and they do good work."

Pratt noticed a small band-aid on the other man's finger. "You're losing your band-aid there."

Frank laughed. "Oh. Thanks. I've got this wart. I'm trying a natural cure." He laughed at himself. "Nothing else seems to work."

Pratt took the card and stuffed it into his pocket. "Thanks. I appreciate it." He started to turn away, counting on the man's guilt or curiosity to stop him. It would give him an excuse to discuss the break-in without raising suspicion.

He wasn't disappointed.

"So do the police have any idea who it was?"

Pratt plastered a confused look on his face. "Who what was?"

"The thief."

"Oh, as far as we can tell nothing was taken."

Frank's eyes widened just slightly. "Really? That's strange. Why would someone break in and not take anything?"

Pratt did his best Becky impersonation, shrugging. "I think Anna disturbed him before he could finish what he was there for. I don't think he was your normal, everyday thief though."

"Oh yeah? Why's that?"

"He trashed her office but didn't touch anything in the store. He seemed to be looking for something specific."

Frank shook his head. "You don't expect that kind of thing in Crocker. It's a shame." He clapped Pratt on the shoulder again, dismissing him with a smile. "You bring that door in and I'll make sure the glass gets repaired ASAP."

Pratt walked the rest of the aisles before returning to Becky and paying for his purchases. There were no other customers in the store. Which meant, unless somebody went out the front door while he was talking to Frank, whoever it was had left through the back. The manager hadn't been wearing an apron so it was possible he wasn't one of Anna's whispering conspirators. But if he wasn't, who was?

He pushed open the door and walked outside, handing Anna a giant candy bar. "I didn't know how much of a chocolate fix you needed.

She grinned widely. "Score! I would never have bought the giant size, but since *you* bought it, I can eat it without guilt."

He laughed, ushering her toward the car. "Did you see anybody?"

"Nobody came out the front door. How about you? Any luck?"

He opened her car door and waited for her to climb inside, then walked around and slid into the driver's side before answering. As he told her about his conversation with

Frank she sat quietly, staring out the front window with her chocolate bar clutched in her hand.

When he'd finished, she turned, fixing him with an intense green gaze. "So, what do you think? Was he involved?"

"I'm not sure. He could be a really good liar. I think it's strange that he didn't ask the obvious question when I gave him the opening."

"What question?"

"What could a pretty, young antiques store owner have in her office that someone would break in to steal?"

Her cheeks turned pink at his characterization of her. "Maybe he assumed they were looking for money."

"Maybe. Or maybe he already knew what the intruder was looking for." Either way, Pratt found it strange he didn't ask.

***

Anna had Pratt stop by the post office so she could finally mail the bills she'd been trying to pay when her store had gotten broken into. By the time they got to the store, there was a big, black SUV parked in front, right next to the yellow curb that declared the space a no parking zone. The vanity plate read, IRaSs.

"Well, they got the ass part right," Pratt said.

As Anna unlocked the front door, a man climbed out of the SUV. He wore a black suit, a crisp white shirt, and dark, wrap-around sunglasses.

Pratt murmured, "We either have aliens in the neighborhood, or the government is paying us a visit."

Anna frowned. "Aliens?" She turned around as the door swung open. "Oh." She laughed. "Men in Black. Got it." She just had time to settle her purse behind the counter before the black-suited man opened the door, setting the bell on the door to jangling.

Bess was perched on the end of the counter, her long legs crossed and one foot bouncing energetically. "Who's the hoister?"

"Can I help you?" Anna asked.

The man sauntered closer, his stride screaming arrogance. "Are you the owner of this establishment, Miss?"

She came around the counter and offered him her hand. "I am. Anna Yesterday. And you are?"

"IRS. We received an anonymous report that you are doing a cash business and not reporting some of your earnings. I'm afraid we're going to have to audit your books."

She glanced at Pratt, heat flooding her face. "That's not true. I keep very careful records."

"Good. Then you shouldn't have a problem showing them to me."

Pratt stepped forward. "Can I see the report?" He might have been a specter too, judging by the way Mr. Man in Black ignored him.

"You want me to knock this dandy into a cocked hat?" Bess asked. The ghost blipped and she was suddenly standing next to the government goon, her body pressed toward his as she glared up at him. "He's nothin' more'n codfish aristocracy. I'd cotton the chance to gouge out his eyes and glue 'em to the outside of those peeper protectors."

Anna murmured, "Don't tempt me."

The man slipped his glasses off, showing her hostile, blue eyes. "Excuse me?"

Pratt moved between IRS and Anna, forcing the smaller man to take a step back. "There is no excuse for coming into an honest businesswoman's place of business and accusing her of breaking the law. Now, unless you're going to produce the report, verifying her accuser, we have nothing more to talk about and you should leave."

The man stared down his long nose at Pratt, no easy task since Pratt was a full three inches taller. IRS twisted his lips as if he were looking at a steaming pile of dog poop on his shoe. "Maybe you didn't hear me. I said I'm IRS. As in backed by the full power and force of the government."

"Yeah. I heard you and, despite the government's best efforts, this is still a free country and business owners still have some rights. Now, you've informed the lady that she is to be audited. I suggest you leave your card and she'll call for an appointment when it's convenient."

The man stared at Pratt a moment longer and then shrugged, sliding a card from his pocket. He handed it to Anna. "I look forward to seeing you very soon, ma'am. Don't make me come looking for you again."

Pratt followed the man to the door and stood watching him, all but daring him to return. "Nice license plate, IRS. It definitely suits you."

IRS frowned. Apparently, he wasn't pleased by the plate. It must have hit a little too close to home. Anna wondered who'd saddled him with it.

Pratt didn't leave the doorway until the black SUV was pulling away from the curb. "What an ass."

She nodded, biting her lip. Tears burned her eyes and it made her mad. "I'll be in my office. I guess I need to start pulling my records together for an audit." She started toward the back room.

"Anna."

She didn't stop walking. All she wanted to do was get to her office before she burst into tears.

"Did it occur to you this might have something to do with Mason Bethesda?"

She stopped, turned around, and felt the tears draining away under a wave of anger. "The timing *is* very suspicious isn't it?"

"Yup. And if it *is* him, we'll make it go away once we figure out what's going on. Unless things have changed drastically since I was a cop, harassment is still illegal."

"I hope you're right."

"I'm right. Believe me, I've dealt with guys like Bethesda before. He's cornered and he'll try just about anything to keep from going down. You leave this to me. I'll do some digging and find out if the IRS thing is just a scare tactic. At the very least I'll make sure you don't have to deal with Mr. IRaSs if you do have to go through an audit."

Finally, she smiled. He was absolutely right. And she was willing to trust him to make things right. In fact, Anna realized, she was beginning to think Pratt Davies could do just about anything he set his mind to. And she was also finding out that he was sorely wasted at Yesterday's Antiques.

CHAPTER NINE

"Where's the cowboy? He promised he'd help me with my bike."

Pratt and Anna shared a look. "He had to go away for a while," Anna told the boy.

"Away?" Pierce exclaimed. "But he promised to help." Pierce started to fidget, tugging on his shirt and looking around the room as if Joss were just hiding.

"I can help you until he gets back," Pratt offered. "I'm sure he'll be back very soon." His gaze held Anna's as he said the words, making it clear who he'd really meant them for.

She smiled gratefully. "I thought we'd paint the bike today, Pierce. Does that sound like fun?"

"I don't like brushes. Brushes hurt my fingers." Pierce stood frowning at the bike as if he blamed it for Joss's disappearance."

"Then you're in luck." Pratt grabbed a can off the worktable. "Because we're not going to use brushes, we're going to use spray paint."

Pierce redirected his frown to the can in Pratt's hand. "That opening is far too small to get a brush into. It will take a very small brush. I don't like small brushes either."

Pratt sprayed the paint over the drop cloth they'd spread beneath the bike. "No brushes. See?" He offered Pierce the can. "Here, you want to try?"

Pierce suddenly eyed the can as if it had bacteria. "You touched the can. I can't touch the can now."

Pierce indicated a pair of rubber gloves on the worktable. "You won't be touching the can, only the gloves will touch the can, and nobody will touch the inside of the gloves but you."

Anna expelled a breath, squeezing Pratt's arm as she left them. Pratt might have started off on Pierce's wrong side, but he was quickly figuring out the pitfalls and avoiding them nicely. "I'll just go call Heather and tell her Pierce will be staying until lunchtime."

Pierce was spraying blue paint over the drop cloth in arcs and circles. "Tell her I'll be home at exactly noon. And I'll have my usual. On Sundays, I have grilled cheese without the crusts. On Mondays, I have tuna fish, on brown bread, with the crusts…"

Anna left Pratt to experience Pierce's weekly menu and headed for her office, thinking she had a new respect for Heather Johnson. Dealing with an extremely bright autistic son must be a daunting proposition. Even so, Pierce had a definite charm and Anna was going to enjoy having him around.

She called Heather and told her that Pierce was settling in well and would be home at noon. Then she hung up and started trying to clean up the mess her intruder had left behind. She placed a pile of brochures back on top of the safe, feeling her heart take a painful lurch when she thought about Joss.

She realized it had been a mistake to use her birthday as the code for the safe. If she'd shown a little more initiative, Joss probably would never have been stolen. Anna doubted the person who'd breeched her safe had been a professional thief. Though the influx of new people in town due to New Crocker made it a slightly better possibility than it would have been a year or two earlier. Still, she had a strong suspicion it was somebody she knew. Somebody who had been living in Crocker nearly fifty years earlier, when the previous mayor got himself embroiled in a scandal that he'd had to take drastic measures to quash.

The front doorbell jangled, and Anna happily took a break from re-organizing papers into the filing cabinet. Brushing her hands together, she left her office and headed for the front, glancing at Pratt on the way through. "I'll take care of this."

He nodded and returned to his task of pounding dents out of the bike's bumpers. She noticed he was wearing a pair of the rubber gloves and smiled. Pierce was applying spray paint to the bike frame like a persnickety Picasso.

The man standing just inside the door, looking around, wore a brown uniform with a set of keys embroidered on the front. The name, *Handi-Locks* was in white above the keys. She extended a hand as she approached. "Hello, I'm Anna Yesterday."

"Scott Friese." The fifty-some-year-old, slightly overweight locksmith shook her hand. "I understand you need new locks for the doors."

"Yes, please. And I'd like an extra deadbolt installed on both doors too. Can you do that today?"

"I think I have what I need on the truck. It will take a couple of hours longer though."

"That's fine. Let me show you the back door. As soon as you're done with it we need to take it to the hardware store to have the glass replaced so if you can do that door first I'd appreciate it."

"No problem." They passed through the workroom and the locksmith nodded at Pratt and greeted the boy. "Hey, Pierce."

Pierce glanced up from his masterpiece, which probably had two inches of blue paint on it at that point, and responded to Mr. Friese' greeting. "Hello, Mr. Friese."

Seeing Anna's look of surprise at the exchange, Friese explained, "Pierce's mom brings him into Gilfer's a lot. I'm in there all the time because I get most of my supplies from Frank Gilfer."

She showed him the door, which sported a piece of plywood over the window area. "You and Frank know each other pretty well then?"

Friese dropped to one knee, carefully examining the lock. "We've known each other for years. Since grade school."

"Really?" Her mind spun with questions. "I guess these days he's running the hardware store for his dad, huh?"

Friese snorted. "Thank goodness." He blinked, seeming to realize what he'd said. "Sorry. That wasn't nice was it?"

She tightened her lips to keep from smiling. "It's okay. I ran into old Mr. Gilfer this morning. I totally understand. I'm guessing he'd be difficult to work with."

Scott straightened, writing the number of the lock on a small notepad in his hand. "Difficult would be a vacation." The locksmith shook his head. "He didn't use to be that way. His dad and my dad were friends and I guess he was a pretty decent guy once upon a time."

"What happened?"

"Not sure. But whatever it was, it made him bitter and angry." Scott stuffed the pad in his pocket and smiled. "I'll just go get my stuff and we'll have this door fixed up in a jiffy."

Anna nodded. Then she thought of one more question. "Mr. Friese?"

He stopped and turned back. "Yes?"

"Do you know when Mr. Gilfer changed?"

Friese frowned. "No. But my dad could probably fill you in." He cocked his head. "Why do you ask?"

Too late, she realized how strange her question must have sounded to him. Thinking fast, she came up with a fairly plausible explanation that would help her with any future questions she might have to ask. "I…well…don't tell anybody." She smiled. "Since my business relies heavily on the past, I thought it would be fun to write a history of Crocker and sell it here in the store. I'm gathering information about all the original business owners."

Friese frowned and Anna held her breath, hoping he bought her story.

"I think that's a great idea." He finally said. "My dad would be thrilled to give you information about the town. He's been a member of the Chamber of Commerce for twenty years and knows just about everything there is to know about the businesses in Crocker."

"Oh, that would be very helpful."

Anna waited as Friese scribbled something on a page of his small notebook and tore it off, handing it to her. "My dad's phone number. He's usually at home most nights."

"Thank you, Mr. Friese."

"Scott. Please." His smile had turned a bit warmer with the news that she was going to write a book about local businesses. She realized that the book would be great advertising for anyone she featured. Feeling guilty for having lied to the locksmith, she said, "Of course I'd like to talk to you too. Sometime soon. About Handi-Locks."

"Any time." He bounced happily out of the store, heading for his truck.

Anna turned to find Bess, hands on hips and a glare on her over-painted face. "Oh, hi Bess. What do you want? I'm kind of busy."

"I want you to give a dash about Jossy instead of cavortin' around with every no-account in town."

With one eye on Pratt and Pierce, who were chatting amiably as they worked, Anna spoke in a harsh whisper. "Believe me I'm doing everything I can. I want Joss back as badly as you do." She suddenly realized she'd forgotten to ask Bess about the article. "I'm glad you're here. Do you remember a story about the Mayor attacking one of his maids? From 1964?"

The ghost frowned. "Are you crazy as a loon? What does that have to do with findin' Jossy?"

"It's the reason his binding object was taken. If I can find the gun belt, I'll find him."

Bess's scowl softened slightly. "No. I don't recollect nothin' about that. I ain't in on your designs. I can't help less'n you're fixin' to fill me in."

The front doorbell jangled, signaling Friese's return. Anna spoke quickly and quietly. "I'm sorry, Bess. You're right. I'll try to keep you in the loop from here on out."

Friese walked into the workshop just as the front door jangled again. Anna looked at Bess, lifting her eyebrows. "I promise we'll talk later." She gave Scott Friese a smile as she passed him on the way back out front.

***

"Who's the clown lady?"

Pratt glanced at Pierce. "What?"

The boy frowned. "The lady wearing the funny, ruffled dress that's all hiked up on one side. My mom would say she was dressed like a street walker. But I wouldn't say that because that wouldn't be respecting my elders."

Pratt turned around and saw the man from Handi-Locks heading toward the door with a large toolbox. The man set the box down on the floor in front of the door and rubbed his arms, looking at the ceiling as if trying to find the source of whatever had chilled him. "I think that's Bess. Where is she standing exactly?"

Pierce lowered his spiky, dark eyebrows in a frown. "Don't your eyes work right? I have perfect eyesight. I passed the test at school and don't have to get glasses. Maybe you need glasses, Mr. Pratt."

"Just call me Pratt, Pierce."

"Okay, Pratt Pierce. Hey, your last name is the same as my first name!" The caterpillar-like eyebrows climbed north as Pierce smiled. He set the can of blue paint on the table and stepped back, plucking at his paint-smeared shirt with paint-coated gloves.

"Very funny. Just tell me where the lady is standing. I can't see her."

Pierce lifted a hand and pointed vaguely in the direction of the locksmith, his gaze averted. "I can't look at her because she has abundant cleavage. I'm not supposed to have sexual feelings about women. My mom will know if I do and I'll be chastised."

Pratt stared at Pierce, having no idea where to go with the boy's last statement. Finally, he just shook his head and turned away, heading toward the locksmith. The man turned as he approached and Pratt offered his hand. "Mr. Friese, I'm Pratt Davies. I called you this morning."

"Mr. Davies. Thanks for the business."

"My pleasure. Frank Gilfer recommends you highly."

Friese dropped his hammer into the toolbox. "He told me to expect your call."

"Oh, you talked to him?"

"I was in the store this morning and I ran into Frank."

Pratt smiled. "We must have just missed each other."

"I wouldn't have seen you anyway, most likely. I was in the back room with Susan. She had some safes for me to open."

Pratt's eyes widened. "You open safes?"

"It's part of my service. Owners sometimes forget the combinations on their safes so I refit them."

"I'm surprised you do them at the store instead of on site."

"Gilfers takes in the small safes and I open them in the store. They give me a list of the larger or fitted ones and I do those jobs onsite."

Pratt nodded. "I wouldn't think you'd get much call for that in a town like Crocker."

He laughed. "You'd be surprised."

A few minutes later, his mind spinning with possibilities, Pratt thanked the locksmith again and went to help Pierce put a new horn on his bike.

CHAPTER TEN

The door opened and a woman came inside. She moved over to the cheap, ugly desk and settled a small, rectangular, canvas bag on top. Joss stood behind her and watched as she shoved the chair back and crouched down in front of the desk. She reached into the leg well and worked until Joss heard a click. He moved closer, looking over her shoulder.

As the door to what he could now see was a safe opened, a wave of something that felt like home slid over him. Joss just barely resisted the urge to shove her brutally aside to get to whatever was in that safe. He had a feeling he knew what it was.

But violence against women was not in his makeup. If it was, he'd have clocked Bess a few decades ago. The woman placed the flat, canvas packet inside the safe, closed the door, and spun the dial before standing.

Shoving the chair back underneath the desk, the woman fussed with some papers, picked up a dirty coffee mug, and turned around. She stopped mere inches from Joss and blinked, stilling like a deer at the first scent of a hunter. Her eyes widened, scanning the small room nervously, and she clasped a hand over her throat. Joss could see her pulse beating a sharp staccato at the side of her pale throat. Her eyes fell on the open door. "Who's there?"

"I am." Joss told her, giving her a little finger wave like he'd seen Anna do a hundred times over the years. The thought speared his heart with sadness. What if he never saw her again?

The woman jumped a little and for a moment he thought she'd heard him. But then she shook her head and, rubbing her hands down her arms, walked right through him to the door. She shuddered, turned back one more time, and then left, leaving the door open.

Joss headed straight for that door and tried to follow, but at the doorframe he bumped up against an invisible barrier. Apparently, he wasn't going anywhere. He peered through the opening and saw a vast expanse of blackness, filled with large, ungainly shapes that looked like machinery and boxes. High on the outside walls, a couple of smudged and cracked windows showed the low light of dusk or dawn. He didn't recognize anything about the place. It even smelled different.

The woman stopped at the bottom of the stairs, gave a sigh, and turned back around, returning to the door where Joss stood with slow, reluctant steps. "I hate this dang place," she murmured. Then she grabbed the edge of the door and slammed it shut in Joss's face.

He returned to pacing the twelve by twelve dimensions of his cell. There had to be some way to get back to Yesterday's Antiques. And by dang, he decided, he was gonna find it!

***

Anna locked the front door and flipped the *Open* sign to *Closed*. She glanced at Pratt as he emerged from the back room.

"Door's all snug again." He handed her the key for the new deadbolt. "You need to make sure this isn't within reaching distance of the door, in case the glass gets broken again."

She frowned. He was alluding to another break-in. "Thanks, Pratt. Hopefully that won't be an issue."

He nodded. "I added security stickers to all the doors and windows too. Sometimes that's all it takes to keep thieves away."

Nodding, Anna rubbed her arms. She gave him a hesitant smile. "I'd like to talk to Mr. Friese tonight. Can you come with me?"

"Can we do it tomorrow night? I have something else I need to do tonight." His gaze flicked to the door, the counter, the windows. He reached out and touched a display, straightening it slightly.

Anna realized he was avoiding her gaze. "Okay, what aren't you telling me?"

"Nothing. Why do you ask?"

Anna crossed her arms. "I'm not letting you go until you fess up. What do you have planned for tonight?"

"Okay, you got me. I thought I'd go over and see what I can find out about the paper."

"I already asked about the article there. All it got me was a couple of visits by Mason Bethesda. Besides, and I checked, the publisher of the paper during that time is dead. He died about fifteen years ago."

"I wasn't planning on going to the newspaper office."

Anna started to shake her head and then stopped as she realized what he had in mind. "You're going to the printing plant?"

He stared at her for a minute and then sighed, nodding.

"Why? What do you hope to find there?"

"I had the idea this morning, when I was watching you write out yesterday's transactions in your little log book."

Her cheeks heated. "I know it's stupid, with the computer and all, but I like having a hard record of my business."

He shook his head. "I don't think that's stupid, but that wasn't where I was going. It occurred to me that, in the old days that would have been the only way for the plant manager to keep track of things."

Her eyes widened. "You're right! They would have logged every news story, every print run."

"Yep."

"Genius. Now all we have to do is pray they kept all those logs."

"Newspapers keep everything."

Anna frowned. "You think you can get past the plant manager?"

"Not without getting hinky." His golden-brown eyes sparkled. "But *you* probably could."

***

"I know I'm going to regret letting you talk me into this."

Pratt pulled the black knit cap down over his light brown hair and grinned. "Hey, you got the easy part. I have to sneak around like a thief and try not to get caught."

"If you get caught, just tell them you were looking for me."

"You have everything you need?"

Anna patted her pockets and pulled out her cell phone, showing him the text she'd typed out, ready to send to give him the all clear. "I have my notebook and my pepper spray too. Just in case."

He nodded. "Don't forget to make sure the door is unlocked."

Clasping her trembling hands together, Anna said, "I can't believe I'm doing this."

Pratt stepped closer, until he was standing just a few inches away. His gaze held hers. A smile lighting his eyes, he reached out and rubbed his fingertip over the end of her nose. "You had a little ink just there."

His mouth curved and she found her gaze being drawn to the wide, sensual lips. "Um…okay. Here goes."

Pratt dipped his head and touched those exquisite lips to hers. Anna's breath locked in her lungs and her body stilled.

Her sensual core tightened under the delicious touch. When he pulled away, she swallowed hard. "That was for luck," he said.

Her legs wobbly, Anna nodded and turned away, barely resisting the urge to reach up and touch her lips with a shaky finger. She felt warm and fuzzy all over from the kiss. But as she approached the wide, low-slung building squatting under the yellow glow of the security lights, her thoughts returned to the terrifying reality of what she was about to do.

It wasn't going to be nearly as much fun as that kiss. In fact, it wasn't even in the same ballpark.

The dented metal door to the print facility was locked. The sign on the door proclaimed the name of the facility, Quality Print, and the hours it was open to the public. Anna didn't need to look at her watch to know she was beyond those hours. She rang the bell attached to the side of the door and waited.

Nothing.

She rang it again and turned around, looking for Pratt in the shadows. She didn't see him anywhere. The door swung open behind her and Anna jumped guiltily, swinging around and reaching for the pepper spray in her pocket.

A man stood inside the door, his overalls stained with ink. "Can I help you?"

Anna forced a smile onto her face. "Hello, I'm Anna Yesterday. I had an appointment with Cliff Young."

The man frowned. "The plant manager has gone home for the day, ma'am. You must be mistaken."

Anna opened her notebook and perused it. "No, I wrote the time and date down, see?" She turned it around and held it up for the man inside the facility to see. "He was going to give me a tour of the plant. You see I'm thinking of printing my book here."

He shook his head. "I'm sorry, you'll have to reschedule. His daughter had a soccer game tonight. He won't be back until the morning."

Relieved she wouldn't have to try to convince the plant manager that he'd made an appointment he really hadn't, Anna gave the man standing in the door her best impression of a disappointed face. "Dang it! If I don't do it tonight, I won't be able to do it for a few weeks. I'm leaving town in the morning." She sniffed, digging in her pocket for a tissue and using it to dab at her eyes. "That's why he agreed to see me on a Sunday night."

The man glanced back inside as if wishing he could escape. "He must have forgotten about the game. I'm sorry." He started to step back, pulling the door closed as he retreated."

Anna panicked, "No, wait!" Her hand shot out and wrapped around the frame so he couldn't close it without pinching her fingers. "Couldn't *you* give me the tour? I promise I won't ask a lot of questions. I just want to look at the place where my book will be printed before I sign the contract."

The man wavered so she went in for the kill. "Please? You'd be my hero." She gave him a watery grin that he seemed unable to withstand. He finally nodded. "I can't give you much time, but I'll give you a quickie."

Anna barely kept from grimacing at the image. "I appreciate this so much." She stepped through the door and it closed with a bang behind her. She glanced around at the door, realizing it locked automatically.

"Come on. I'll show you the presses."

Anna looked at the door again, trying to think of a way to unlock it without him noticing. She couldn't come up with anything.

"Are you coming?"

Anna forced a smile and fell in behind him, feeling as if the walls were closing in on her. "So," she asked him as they walked from the shadows by the door into a well-lighted space filled with printers, "—are you here all by yourself tonight?"

"Yeah. On Sunday nights we run lean. Sometimes Mr. Young's here with me but…well, I already told you about his daughter's game." He threw a smile over his shoulder.

Anna reached into her pocket and sent the "all clear" text to Pratt, hoping he could find a way inside the locked building.

***

Pratt tested the door handle and found it locked. *Dangit!* He sighed. He hadn't wanted to do it, but he'd have to resort to Plan B. Pratt used his lock pick set to open the door and ducked inside. He eased the door closed and stepped back into the shadows to scope out the immediate area. He heard voices coming from deep inside the facility but nothing else.

Keeping to the shadows as much as possible, Pratt scooted along the wall, looking for an office or an archive area. He hoped Anna was able to keep the printer engaged for a few more minutes anyway. Pratt would take every minute she could give him.

He found the office and it was unlocked. A quick search told him there were no logs and the ancient computer was too old and slow to store much. He moved to the next room in the hall and discovered a storage area filled with boxes. Using his flashlight instead of turning on the overhead light, Pratt did a visual scan of the boxes and didn't see anything that looked promising, so he moved on.

The next two doors led to restrooms. He moved past them and found another office, which looked like it belonged to a woman. He did find some old logs tucked into the back of the closet in that room but they appeared to be design notes. No printer's logs.

He returned to the hallway and headed for the last door. A cold, musty smell assailed him as he opened the door and his nose twitched. Decay was not Pratt's friend. He had severe mold allergies. Tamping down on the sneeze dancing at the edge of his sinuses, Pratt started down the steps. They were slimy with moisture, the wood slick under his shoes. He held onto the rusted, metal railing to keep from slamming down the stairs on his ass.

At the bottom he stopped, sent his flashlight around the small, dark space, and sighed. There was a stack of boxes piled up against one damp wall. He'd have to go through them all. Pratt settled his flashlight on top of a box and used one of his lock pick tools to tear through the tape sealing another.

The box was filled with rolls of old printer paper. The next box held bottles of something black, like ink or primer. He moved the top boxes to the floor and opened the next box. Ripping it open, he saw a bunch of tubes with tattered, ink-smudged edges. Inside each tube was a roll of paper. Pratt reached for one of the tubes, tugging it upward. The soft scuff of a shoe had him turning his head and a bright light flashed in his eyes, making him squint and duck his head.

Pain lanced through his skull as the light swung sideways. He took a glancing blow since he'd been ducking at the time the flashlight swung. Pratt hit the cold, clammy concrete, barely catching himself on his hands to keep his head from cracking against the hard surface.

Soft footfalls sounded against the concrete and Pratt started to push off, intending to launch himself at his attacker. But he didn't have time. The flashlight swung in an arc and pain exploded once again. He didn't even feel the ground coming up to meet him.

CHAPTER ELEVEN

"Quality does the printing for two dailies, five weeklies, and an assortment of advertising companies. We also take on the occasional special project, like your book."

Anna eyed the massive printers that dominated the room. "These look fairly new." She was barely listening to the printer's spiel. All she could think about was whether Pratt had been able to find a way inside.

The man, who'd introduced himself as Jeff Sundy, nodded proudly. "The owner replaced all the old machines last year."

"That had to have cost a fortune. Business must be good."

Sundy shrugged. "I don't know much about the business end of things. I just do the printing."

Anna nodded and listened for a few more minutes while the man explained how they set the print area, loaded the paper, and controlled the output of the big machines. It was all Greek to her. "Where do you store the projects? Are they in a safe place?"

"Oh yes. We have a server located in a remote datacenter. They back up the information regularly so there's redundancy."

"This facility has been around for a while hasn't it? I read somewhere that it was built in the nineteen fifties."

"Yeah. Old Buck Stevens started out with just a rusty old metal building and he's turned it into quite a goldmine." Sundy laughed. "We always joke about him havin' the Midas touch."

"It sure seems that way." She smiled. "What about those early projects, from when the plant opened? Where do you keep that information?"

He frowned and it was clear he wondered why she asked.

"I'm just nosy. I deal in antiques so I live in the past." She laughed, hoping her offhand manner would put his suspicions at rest.

"Oh, yeah. I know how that can be. We didn't start storing information digitally until the late 1970s. Before that I don't know. We used lithographers." He shrugged.

"Fascinating. How did that work?"

"Obviously, that was before my time. But I have talked to Max Smith and he told me a little about it."

"Max Smith?"

"He was the lithographer when Quality first opened its doors. He's really old now and about half senile, but he used to come to all the company picnics and he was really interesting to talk to."

"He hasn't been around lately?"

"He might be dead." Sundy shrugged. "He's been out at Happy Acres for years."

Anna nodded. "How did the stories get printed back then?"

"Plates. It was quite an art, really. Guys like Max would get the stories from the paper and set them out backward in tiny letters on the plates. I'm not sure how the printing process went after that."

"How did the stories come to Quality? Were they handwritten?"

"Typed on special paper then glued together. Then the stories went to the copy desk for corrections and coding."

"Wow. That sounds like quite a process. I bet you're glad you don't have to set out the pages on plates." Anna laughed.

"You have no idea. I can't even guess how tedious it would be. But dealing with computers can be a challenge too. Some days I think we have gremlins in the system."

"I know exactly what you mean." She smiled. "How did they keep track of the projects they printed?

He shrugged. "I'm guessing it was probably on logs, which would most likely be long gone. If they do still exist the owner might have them. I don't know."

"So, the original owner still owns Quality?"

"He does." Sundy led her across the floor to a small, dark, conference room. Flipping on the light he told her, "This is where you'll pick out all the details for your book. Glynus will help you with that. She's really good with the arty type stuff."

"Great. I look forward to working with her."

Sundy flipped off the light.

"He must be getting pretty old."

The man frowned, "Huh? Who?"

"The owner. If he started Quality in the late fifties, he's got to be what, in his eighties or nineties?"

"Eighties, I think. He was young when he started the company. He didn't do well at first, but when the *Crocker Sun* agreed to let him print the daily newspaper things started to look up."

"Good old American drive and tenaciousness, huh?"

Sundy nodded enthusiastically. "Me and the other employees like to make fun of the old man. He can be a pain in the ass...excuse my French, ma'am...but he's a sharp old coot." Sundy thought for a moment. "You know what, I think Glynus has some brochures about the company in her office. Let me get you one to take with you. There's a really good write-up about Quality, including its history."

Anna nodded enthusiastically. "That would be great, thanks!" As Sundy made his way through the darkened building she looked around for Pratt, hoping he'd found a window he could slide through or another door that wasn't locked. She was tempted to text him again, but was afraid his phone would ding and give him away. So she waited, aware that any time she could give him would help.

When Sundy returned bearing a brochure a moment later he tried to usher her back toward the door. "I need to get to my work now. You caught me just as I was getting ready to start and I'm on a pretty tight schedule."

She stuffed the brochure into her purse. "I understand. Do you mind if I visit the Ladies before I leave? I can find my own way out if you need to get back to work."

"Oh. Sure. It's over there." He pointed toward a dark hallway behind viewing glass. She suspected it was the office area of the building.

"Great. Thanks so much for giving me the tour. It really put my mind at ease."

"I'm happy I could help. 'Night now." Anna watched him saunter away before hurrying toward the offices. Maybe she could find Pratt in there. It seemed a logical place to look for the logs.

Hearing the printers startup, Anna risked calling out softly to Pratt. He didn't respond so she started opening doors, sticking her head inside. "Pratt?"

She didn't find him in any of the rooms. Standing at the end of the hallway, she frowned, worried. What if he hadn't been able to get through the door?

A hand covered Anna's mouth and she screamed, the sound muffled by the hand and swallowed up in the sounds of printing coming from the main room. She fought her assailant desperately, flailing her legs as she was pulled backward, into musty smelling blackness. The hand over her face smelled like salad dressing, making Anna's stomach roil. The person holding her was strong and much bigger than she was. Despite her best efforts, he dragged her none too gently down a set of slimy stairs, her heels scraping against the wood.

Anna's assailant dragged her across the darkened room at the bottom of the stairs and threw her against some boxes. She started to turn, her arm coming around to shove him to the side, but she stumbled against something warm and solid on the ground and fell to her hands and knees.

She gave a horrified little squeal and tried to scramble backward, off the body on the floor. By the time she shoved herself clear her mind finally registered Pratt's familiar sandalwood scent, overlaying the stench of stagnant air in the underground space.

She was vaguely aware of a door slamming shut in the distance as she scrambled back to Pratt, her hands sliding over him as she spoke his name. She shook him gently and he groaned, rolling to his back.

She placed a hand on his face. "Are you hurt?"

Pratt lay on his back for a minute without speaking. His hand lifted to his head and he sucked in air as his fingers connected. "Just a couple of bumps on my head." He started to sit up. "How'd you find me?"

Anna helped him sit. "Apparently we have a mutual friend. I think he locked us down here."

She couldn't see Pratt's features in the dark, but she could tell by the sudden squaring of his shoulders when he'd shaken off his fogginess. Pratt touched her hand. "He didn't hurt you, did he?" There was something in his tone of voice—an underlying trace of steel—which made her stomach do a little flip. "I'm fine. He didn't do anything except drag me down here."

Pratt's head bobbed once in a nod. "Good. Okay, so we need to get out of here and then figure out who's responsible." He shoved to his feet, groaning softly, and patted his pockets. "Ha! I still have it. Let's go."

Pratt reached out and Anna placed her hand in his. "Where are we going?"

"Out of here."

"But the door's locked."

"Whoever hit me on the head didn't think to search me. I still have my lock pick."

She stopped, feeling panic sliding through her at his words. "You...you have a lock pick?" At that moment she realized she didn't really know anything at all about Pratt. She'd taken his word for the fact that he'd been a cop and hadn't bothered to verify his references. Her friends and family had always told her she was too trusting. "Where'd you get that?" Her muscles tightened and nausea flared.

"On the Internet. Now come on, let's get out of this basement before the guy who put us here comes back."

That was enough of an impetus to get her moving again. The memory of those rough hands dragging her, covering her mouth... Anna shuddered.

***

It took Pratt a little more time than he'd expected to open the door. His flashlight was broken so he had to do it strictly by feel. But finally, the lock gave and he opened the door a crack, peering into the relatively light area of the hallway above.

In the distance, the sound of the printing presses droned on, covering any other sounds pretty effectively. He opened the door a few more inches and went through, reaching back for Anna's hand. When she came through the door, he leaned down and whispered into her ear. "Straight to the exit. No stops. Keep your eyes peeled the whole way in case our mutual friend is still skulking around."

She nodded sharply. Her pretty face looked gray in the weak light from the printer room and her eyes looked huge. Her hand felt small and cold in his. A wave of tenderness slipped through him and, for a beat in time, he wavered on the edge of kissing her. Anything to take the look of stark terror off her face. But the need for speed had him moving forward, hurrying toward the front door.

As they left the office section of the building, Pratt slammed to a stop, backtracking to stay in the shadowed hallway. A few feet ahead of them, blocking the door, two figures stood talking. It was too dark to see who they were, but one of them was gesticulating wildly, apparently very upset. The other man stood with sloped shoulders, chin low, and appeared to be listening without comment.

Pratt briefly considered confronting them. He was a pretty good street fighter and he knew from the way his and Anna's confinement had been managed that he wasn't dealing with pros. But there was Anna's safety to be considered. And he wasn't willing to risk her being harmed. So he turned and placed a finger over his lips, starting off in the opposite direction. There had to be a back door to the facility. He only hoped it wasn't tied to an alarm system because they'd be a lot farther from the car on that side.

Halfway down the hall he jerked to a stop. He'd heard a voice coming from the printer floor. Pratt dropped into a crouch, pulling Anna with him. After a moment he realized he was only hearing one side of a conversation being conducted in a very loud voice. He straightened slightly and looked out over the floor.

The man who'd opened the door to Anna was standing by the machine, adjusting buttons on the printer console and talking on his cell phone. When the man turned his back to them, Pratt grabbed Anna's hand again and sprinted the rest of the way down the hall.

As hoped, they found a back exit around the corner at the end of the hall and Pratt wasted no time shoving the bar to open it. They emerged into a clear, star-studded night and the energetic sound of crickets. Easing the door slowly closed, Pratt quietly celebrated the broken security light that left them in darkness. He pulled Anna into a run and they made it back to his car, which he'd parked at the far edge of the parking lot, tucked under a large tree so it wasn't visible.

Pratt didn't speak until they were on the road, heading back toward town. He became aware that Anna was being very quiet and he attributed it to the easing of adrenalin from their little adventure. He felt really guilty about that. "Listen,

Anna. I'm sorry I dragged you into that mess. I should have known better."

She didn't respond. Staring straight ahead, she twisted her fingers together and sat stone still. Pratt figured she must really be mad at him. "Anna? Are you ever going to talk to me again?"

She blinked, turning her head slowly. "Pratt, tell me about your past."

Horror made his palms go damp on the steering wheel. "I…told you about it…when you hired me."

She shook her head. "Not really. You just told me you'd been a cop in St. Louis and you were looking for a change. I don't know anything about you. Nothing at all."

She looked so worried Pratt really wished he could tell her what she wanted to hear. But he couldn't do that. "It's not a very interesting story. I graduated from Washington University, after four years of working my ass off to get a degree I couldn't really use, and decided I wanted to be a cop. I wanted to be part of the solution instead of being part of the problem." He shrugged.

"What about your family?"

He frowned. "My family? What about them?"

"Do you have any sisters or brothers?"

His hesitation was brief. He hoped she didn't notice it. "No."

They sat in tension-fraught silence for a moment. Finally, Pratt added. "I had a sister once. She's gone now."

He hadn't wanted to make her feel bad. But the side benefit was that she felt guilty enough for prodding him that, after apologizing profusely and tearfully, Anna finally smiled at him again. "Don't apologize, Anna. You couldn't have known. I just don't like to talk about it."

"Is she the reason you stopped being a cop?"

Pratt sucked a surprised breath. He'd known she was smart and intuitive, but he obviously hadn't given her enough credit. "Yes."

With that she seemed willing to drop the subject of his background. Pratt's relief was tempered by a sudden, inexplicable need to share with her. He didn't like lying to the woman he considered a friend at the very least, and could probably love if things were different.

"So, I assume you didn't find any logs?"

"No. Just a bunch of old paper and some chemicals. How about you? Did you learn anything useful?"

She pulled the brochure Sundy had given her out of her pocket. "This has some of the history of the facility. The business was started by a man named Stevens. It appears the early years were rough, but at some point Quality suddenly started to do better and became a thriving business. His employees apparently liked to joke about his Midas touch."

"What's the timing for this good luck?"

"From what Sundy told me, and what's on this timeline in the brochure, I'd say it would have been early sixties."

"The timeline is right."

She nodded. "Sundy said they did use log books, but he figured most of them were gone. He thought the owner might still have some of them."

Pratt's eyebrows lifted at the news. "Sounds like that should be our next stop then, huh?"

CHAPTER TWELVE

Joss hovered next to the window, watching for the artistic boy. He reckoned he could catch the boy's eye as he whizzed by on his moped and get Pierce to tell Anna where he was. Unfortunately, the sidewalks and street were unusually busy and the boy had whipped by without looking his way. Again.

A big, orange tomcat came by and spat at him a few times. The varmint seemed discombobulated by the sight of the specter but it didn't stop him from stalking by every few minutes, whipping his ragged tail and pawing at the glass.

Joss had no idea what had puckered the mangy critter. The feline was considerable beat up. That might be enough to take the chirk out o' anyone, Joss reckoned.

He turned as familiar footsteps sounded on the steps. Joss drifted back to the floor, intending to give the young woman her daily dose of spook mischief. She stopped a few feet from the door, looking all-overish and grum.

"Come on, darlin'. I don't bite. I just moan and rattle my chains."

She frowned.

Joss decided the woman must be a sensitive. She seemed to cotton to his presence in the dingy room. It wouldn't really be all that queer. Anna had. 'Course she'd held his gun belt in her hands. Joss was fair certain the pretty young thing standing in the dark room beyond the door had never held his last earthly possession in her pale hands.

Joss decided to test it. "Come on in, darlin'. I have somethin' I need to ask ya."

She jerked slightly and looked down at the bag. After another moment's thought she turned away and started to leave.

"No!" Joss roared the command and the light bulb over her head rattled in its socket, fracturing the weak yellow light for a moment.

The woman stopped. Her shoulders curved inward as if she were bracing for an attack. Slowly she turned around. "I don't know who you are but I won't hurt you if you don't hurt me. Promise."

"I don't want ta hurt ya, darlin'. I just want to get out of this dang place and get back where I belong."

She stood stock still, her head tilting slightly as if she were listening for something. Joss concentrated on the papers on the desk and sent one skittering through the air toward her.

She jumped back as it fluttered to the ground at her feet. "Crap!" The young woman flung the blue bag toward the door and ran up the stairs, slamming the door hard at the top.

Joss dropped his butt to the edge of the desk and sighed. "Well don't that just cap the climax?"

***

The owner of Quality Print lived in a narrow brownstone overlooking New Crocker. He was surrounded by newly renovated townhouses with perfectly manicured lawns. His yard consisted of sad, brown-tipped grass that gave way to an ever-widening bare patch as it eased toward the house, like male pattern baldness.

Anna and Pratt climbed the wooden stairs to a sagging wooden porch, which was in dire need of a can of white paint.

Pratt looked at Anna. "Let me do the talking."

She lifted her hands and widened her eyes. "Trust me, after last night I've had enough intrigue to last me for a lifetime."

He smiled down at her, unable to resist scraping a silky blonde curl away from her cheek. "It wasn't all bad was it?"

Her cheeks heated and her gaze slid from his as she knocked. After a minute they heard footsteps and Anna dropped back, allowing Pratt to take the lead.

They were surprised when a woman answered the door. She was attractive in an unadorned way and looked to be in her late thirties. "Can I help you?"

Pratt smiled his most winning smile. The woman seemed unaffected, spurring Anna to wonder what was wrong with her. In fact, taking a closer look at her, Anna realized the woman appeared nervous. Her hand on the knob of the screen door was shaking and her dark brown eyes danced between Pratt and Anna as if she expected trouble.

A shout went up across the street and the woman jumped.

Anna turned around and saw that a bunch of young people were gathered on the porch of a popular bar that overlooked the river on the opposite side. "I'll bet it gets a bit noisy here doesn't it?"

The woman didn't acknowledge Anna's attempt at pleasantry. She glanced back toward Pratt. "I'm very busy. Is there something I can help you with?"

"We were hoping we could talk to Mr. Stevens."

"Are you the buyers?"

Pratt's mouth opened and he blinked. Anna touched his arm. "Yes. We wondered if we could talk to him about...the purchase."

Sighing loudly, the woman pushed the screen open and stepped back. "Come on in, then. Gramps isn't here. I haven't set eyes on him for a couple of days. As usual he's left me to deal with everything."

"Aren't you worried about him?" Anna asked the woman.

She shrugged. "Not really. He tends to go off on business trips at a moment's notice and he forgets to tell me. Gramps is set in his ways and he's not good at reporting to someone else." They entered the house and the woman asked them, "Would you like some coffee or something?"

"No. Thank you, though." Pratt smiled. "I take it you're Mr. Stevens's granddaughter?"

She seemed to gather herself and then gave them a tired smile. "I'm sorry. I figured Gramps would have told you about me, since he obviously expected me to handle the sale of Quality." She extended her hand. "I'm Glynus. I'm his granddaughter and partner at the print plant."

"Oh yes. Glynus." Anna took her hand and shook it. "Jeff told me about you."

Glynus Stevens frowned. "You've already met Jeff?"

Too late, Anna realized her mistake. "Oh...I..."

"We might as well fess up, honey." Pratt dropped his arm around her shoulders. "We did a tiny bit of reconnaissance work last night. Anna pretended to be getting a book published so she could get a tour of the place when your grandfather wasn't around. You know, to see if things were the same when he wasn't anticipating an inspection."

Glynus frowned. "Oh. Well, that's irregular."

"It's a lot of money, Miss Stevens. We're very careful people." Pratt told her firmly. "I wouldn't think you'd mind if you didn't have anything to hide."

"I don't have anything to hide, Mr..."

"Just call me Pratt. Please?"

"But I don't know about Gramps. He likes to stretch boundaries."

Anna's eyes widened. It wasn't exactly the kind of thing one would expect a person to say about her grandfather and business partner. Especially to prospective buyers of that business. Deciding to go with her intuition, Anna asked, "I take it you're not happy about the sale?"

Glynus sighed, pointing them to the couch and dropping into an upholstered chair beside the fireplace. "I'm not, no. I love that plant. I grew up there. I spent summer vacations playing among the printers and building forts with copy tubes. As long ago as I can remember I've wanted to work there. And I'm good at the design end of things. Now I'm going to have to find another job and that means moving away from Crocker."

Anna reached over and patted the woman's hand. "I'm sorry. That must be devastating to you. Have you lived here all your life?" Anna knew the answer to that. Glynus Stevens was a decade older than Anna but if she'd grown up in Crocker Anna would have known her. She was simply trying to gain the woman's confidence and draw her out.

"No. We lived in Parkerville. My brother and I used to spend vacations with Gramps though. I only moved here when Gramps asked me to come into the business. Right after college. He said he wanted to leave it to someone and I was the only one in the family with the interest and skill to make a go of it."

"Then why is he selling it now?"

She glanced at Pratt, her fingers twining nervously in the hem of her twinset. "He says he wants to get out of Crocker. He's moving to Florida, I think. And I can't afford to buy it right now. I tried but the bank won't lend that much money to me."

"Couldn't he just let you continue to run the company?"

Glynus seemed to realize suddenly that their questions were strange ones for prospective buyers. She narrowed those aloof, brown eyes on them. "I thought you were interested in buying Quality."

Pratt laughed. "Sorry." He grabbed Anna's hand and kissed the back of it. She felt the impact of that tender kiss all the way to her toes. It was all she could do not to squirm in her seat. "My little Anna is a softie. She can't stand to see anyone sad. I think she'd walk away from the deal if she thought it would put a smile on your face."

The brown gaze softened slightly. "Oh. Well, thanks. But if you don't buy the place someone else will. Gramps is determined to sell it. He says he needs to cut all ties to Crocker." She shrugged. "He's been pretty insistent about it."

"Okay then, we only need one last thing before we make an offer," Pratt told Glynus.

"What's that?"

"We'd like to see any old records you might have on the operation of the facility. Record books, logs, digitized records, things like that."

The woman frowned. "How far back?"

"To the beginning if possible."

"Wow. I'd be surprised if we have records going that far back. But I'll check with Gramps and let you know. I think he's saved some things. I just don't know if he has all of it."

Pratt and Anna stood up and Pratt handed her a business card. "Call me at that number after you've spoken to your grandfather."

Anna took Glynus's hand. "Thank you so much. We're really excited about investing in the plant. We just want to make sure it's a good investment. You understand?"

Glynus shrugged and walked them to the door. "I'll be in touch soon."

***

"Did she seem overly nervous to you?" Pratt asked as he held Anna's door for her.

"She did. It could be because her grandfather is obviously not dependable. I'd be a mess too if somebody dumped the sale of a business on me without warning."

"Maybe." Pratt closed her door and walked around to the driver's side. Sliding into the car, he glanced at Anna. "She did give me an idea for where we need to go next though."

"Where?"

"When she talked about copy tubes, it reminded me that there was a reporter on the other end of that story. If we're lucky he's still alive and he kept his notebooks."

"Or she."

Pratt turned the key. "Or she. Though, in the sixties it would most likely have been a he."

"It will have to wait until this afternoon, though. I need to open the store," she told him.

"Could you do without me for about forty-five minutes?" Pratt asked.

"Of course, why?"

"I thought I'd stop by the police station. Somebody must have gone out to investigate the rape that night."

"You're right. Duh. I hadn't considered that. But since nobody made a stink when the cover-up happened, we can assume whoever it was took a bribe."

"Yup. But maybe I can come at it from another direction."

Anna opened her purse and dug for her keys. "Such as?"

"Such as were any of the police connected to the mayor in some way? Did anybody seem to come into some money around that time? Etc."

"Sounds good." Anna reached for her door as Pratt pulled up in front of Yesterday's. He started to get out to come around but she placed her hand on his knee without thinking. It felt heated and muscular under her fingertips and she jerked her hand away quickly. "Don't move. I got it." She opened the door and climbed out, turning to look at him before closing the door. "See you in a bit?"

His smile made her go all warm and tingly. She closed the door and watched him drive away.

"Well don't you look like the cat that gobbled the canary?"

Anna looked up and saw Heather Johnson approaching. Pierce plodded along behind her with his head down.

She smiled at the older woman. "Hi Heather. Pierce."

Heather waved at Pratt as he drove away. "I was afraid you weren't going to open the store. Pierce would like to bring his bike home today."

"Of course! Hopefully that paint is dry." She looked at the boy, whose gaze was focused on his feet. "You'll be careful with it for a few days, right? You don't want to put a ding in that paint or you'll have to bring it back."

"Will the cowboy help me repaint it?"

Anna opened the door and hurried inside, hoping to pretend she hadn't heard the question. No such luck. Pierce Johnson was as determined as he was opinionated.

"It's rude not to answer a question, Miss Yesterday."

"Pierce!"

Anna set her purse down on the counter, biting her lip. She forced a smile and turned around. "It's okay, Heather, he's right. I was avoiding his question. It's just that this is kind of a sensitive subject with me." She looked at Pierce. "The cowboy is gone, Pierce." Tears stung her eyes and she blinked, trying to dispel them.

The boy's gaze lifted briefly to hers and then skittered away. "Is he coming back? I need to tell him something. He guards the store. He needs to know what I heard. He guards the store."

Heather patted her son on the back and he jerked away. "Don't touch me. I don't like to be touched."

Heather threw Anna an embarrassed look. "I'm sorry. He gets like this sometimes…"

"Don't talk about me like I'm not here, Mother. I'm not deaf. I'm special. You need to treat me like I'm special."

Pierce glared at his mother's torso and she gave Anna a sad smile.

Anna felt her pain. Though he'd been protected to the point that he sometimes seemed younger than his seventeen years, Pierce was smart, inquisitive, and honest. But his honesty could sometimes bruise. "I'm trying really hard to find him, Pierce. I just don't know where to look for him yet."

The boy's gaze slid to Anna's. "I can help look for him. I don't mind."

Anna nodded. "That would be wonderful, Pierce. I'd really appreciate it if you could help. Maybe when you take your afternoon walks you could keep an eye out for him."

"Yes. I can look for him. I want to go look for him right now, Mother."

"What about your bike?"

"I don't want my bike. I want to talk to the cowboy. He needs to know. He guards the store."

Heather frowned, looking at Anna. Anna shrugged. "Pierce, if there's something about the store you should tell Miss Yesterday. She's the owner."

The boy frowned, already turning toward the door. "She's a woman. Women must be protected. The cowboy will know what to do. He guards the store."

Pierce walked over to the door and stood impatiently. He wouldn't pull it open because he'd need to touch the knob. "Come on, Mother!"

Heather touched Anna's hand. "I'm so sorry. I'll try to get him to tell me."

"Thank you." Anna watched them leave, sadness making her chest hurt. She'd been worried about Joss and now she was worried about Pierce. For whatever reason, he'd made a connection with Joss and if, heaven forbid, her favorite cowboy ghost never returned…

She couldn't finish the thought. Her throat tightened and her eyes flooded with tears. No. She couldn't think that way. They had to get Joss back. They just had to.

CHAPTER THIRTEEN

Pratt walked into the Crocker Police building, a low-slung gray brick structure on the edge of town, and walked up to the information window. No one was sitting at the desk behind the window but a paper plate bearing the last bite of a cream cheese covered bagel sat on its top, making it appear as if someone had just left.

He rang the little silver bell and looked around. The room beyond the window had three metal desks in it, none of which held people.

Footsteps finally sounded in the hallway beyond the office and a uniformed cop came through the door, jerking to a stop when he saw Pratt. It was obvious he hadn't known Pratt was there. The cop walked over and shoved the window back. "Sorry, I didn't hear the bell. We're in a meeting right now. Is there something I can help you with? Do you want to report a robbery or something?"

Pratt extended his hand. "I'm Pratt Davies. I wanted to talk to you about a personnel matter."

"Are you a cop?"

"I used to be. But I wasn't trying to apply. I'm helping Anna Yesterday do some research for a book on the history of Crocker and I wanted to ask about a cop who used to work here in the 1960s."

The uniformed cop blinked. "Oh. That was a long time ago." A voice called out from the back of the building and he glanced over his shoulder, responding with, "I'm working." He grinned at Pratt. "You saved me from a really dull meeting. Why don't you fill this out?" He handed Pratt a large tablet with the words, Information Request, across the top. "I'm the Public Liaison for the Crocker PD. I'll see what I can find for you."

Pratt took the tablet and the pen the cop handed him. "Thanks, Officer...?"

"Dresden. Bill Dresden. I heard a private investigator opened shop in New Crocker. Was that you?"

Pratt shook his head. "I'm working down at Yesterday's Antiques. I'm just helping my boss."

Dresden nodded. "So, if you don't mind my askin', why'd you stop being a cop?"

"Pratt smiled. "No. I don't mind. I just got burned out. St. Louis PD can get a little rough."

"Oh, yeah. I bet. He slapped Pratt on the shoulder. Well, if you ever decide to re-up, we can always use a good man here."

"Thanks. I'll keep that in mind." Pratt sat down in the waiting area and filled out the form with as much information as he could. He added his cell phone number so Dresden could call him if he had any further questions. After he handed over the form, there wasn't much left to do but wait. "Thanks for your help, officer."

"Call me Bill. I'll check this out with the Chief. He's been with the Crocker PD since before I was born and before that I think his dad was Chief. He might be able to tell me who you're looking for without much digging."

"That would be great. Thanks again."

Pratt left the PD and headed for the library. He was going to go over some of the same ground Anna had already covered. With his cynicism and training as a cop, he figured he might see something she missed.

With that thought in mind, he parked in front of the library and headed for the microfiche room.

***

Joss hovered in front of the window again, watching for the boy. He'd spent some time earlier in the day preparing a message for the woman. In case she ever returned. It had taken every bit of concentration he had. Like his ability to move around in the place, his power to affect the environment he was in was limited. He figured it was because his remains hadn't been buried beneath the building as they had the antique store.

Regardless, he'd compiled a message he thought would make an impression on her. A flash of orange caught his eye and the cat sauntered into view. It looked at him and spat as usual, but then the big stray walked over to the window and sat down. It stared at Joss through the glass, its scraggly tail snapping with interest. Joss didn't move. He wanted to see what the cat would do. The answer was, not much. It stared at him for another minute, spat again, and started to leave.

He sighed. He was really starting to worry that he would never get back to Yesterday's. If nobody was ever going to see or hear him, he might as well just disappear into mist. But Joss wasn't quite ready to hang up the fiddle yet. He had an idea. But he'd need some help from the woman to accomplish it.

"Oh, my stars!"

He whipped around. He'd been so intent on watching for the boy he hadn't heard her approach. "Hey, darlin'."

Her gaze was riveted on the desktop and his message.

He'd shaped several pens and pencils into the word, "Help". Her gaze left the desktop and slid around the room, slowing when it landed on the window.

Then she frowned. "That darn cat." Suddenly she was moving toward the window, an angry look in her eye. She pulled a chair over and stepped onto it, reaching for the latch. "Shoo! Get lost you scavenger. You've killed your last woodpecker at this house."

The woman pulled the small window open. The cat spat at her and took off. Joss suddenly realized the open window presented a good opportunity for him. If the boy came by, he could call out to catch his attention. When she started to close it he moved close, concentrating on creating a chill that she couldn't miss.

"Why don't you leave that open, darlin'? I'm feelin' a might peevish in this grum room."

She gave a little jerk and cried out, glaring around the room. "Now you look here, whatever you are. I don't know why you're here or what you want from me—"

"I want you to leave the dang window open."

"—but I'm tired of being scared so you and I need to come to an understanding."

Joss crossed his arms over his chest and nodded. "Bully for you, darlin'. It's about time you saw the elephant."

"You're going to leave me alone, and I'll be happy to leave you alone."

Joss snorted. " 'Bout as much chance of that as catchin' a weasel asleep." Joss concentrated on the surface of the desk and lifted the pens, sending them dancing on the air. The woman forgot all about the window and jumped from the chair, heading for the door. But she stopped before she got to it, her hands clenched at her sides. "No. You're not gonna get me again. I came down to put the money in the safe and that's exactly what I'm going to do."

Joss's face split in a smile. "Now don't that just cap the climax?" The pens dropped to the desktop with a clatter. He watched as she grabbed the envelope she'd thrown on the floor the last time she'd been down there and added it to the one she'd carried down with her, heading for the safe. Now all he had to do was figure out how to get her to touch his gun belt while she was in there.

***

The phone rang while Anna was out of the store that afternoon, meeting with a potential client to evaluate some antiques. Pratt picked it up without much thought, his mind on the things he'd discovered at the library. "Yesterday's Antiques."

The voice on the other end of the phone was gruff and soft, nearly inaudible. Pratt had to strain to hear it. "If you want that item from the safe back, bring the clipping to New Crocker tonight at midnight, sealed in a Ziploc, and throw it into the river behind the River Barge Bar. Include any copies you've made. We'll know if it's the real clipping. If this story comes up again, your little girlfriend is going to get hurt. That's a promise."

The call disconnected and Pratt pulled the phone from his ear, his mind spinning. "Dangit!" There would be no way to track the clipping once they put it into the water. The person on the phone could pick it up anywhere along the river, from either side, and they'd be long gone before Pratt could figure out where they were.

To make things worse, the caller had given him no assurance whatsoever that he'd return the gun belt once he had the newspaper. They could be flinging their only insurance into the river and Anna's cowboy might be lost to her forever.

And if he told her to do it, she'd never forgive him.

***

The reporter who wrote the article was still alive. Anna found his name in the Crocker phone book and discovered that he lived just down the street from Glynus Stevens. Both homes overlooked New Crocker and the noise and activity of shops, bars, and restaurants. She remembered when the big, old homes on Jefferson Street had looked out over the picturesque river. The residents couldn't be all that happy about the change.

Pratt had been quiet since returning from the police station that morning. Anna tried to ask him about it but he'd been evasive. He just kept telling her they'd talk about it later, once he had time to digest it. She stood on the reporter's freshly painted porch and watched the constant stream of activity across the street as Pratt knocked on Theodore Miller's door.

When the door opened, Anna found herself looking at a small, perfectly round elderly man with bright eyes, a red face, and stark white hair that badly needed a cut. "Yes?"

Pratt offered the man his hand. "Mr. Miller. I'm Pratt Davies. This is Anna Yesterday. We wondered if we could talk to you about one of your old stories."

The little man smiled at Anna, reaching for her hand and clasping it between his. He smoothed his hand over hers as he held her gaze. He reminded her of a bird, his round, hazel eyes bright with interest. "Miss Yesterday, yes. I know your mama. She moved to the big city, didn't she?"

"Yes. She's living in Indianapolis and really likes it."

He nodded. "It's so nice to see you again. I think you were about five the last time we met."

Anna laughed. "I'm a little taller now, but not much."

The man winked at her. "You look tall to me." He dropped her hand and pulled the door closed. "We can sit out here. Would you like some iced tea?"

"No. Thank you. We're fine." Pratt lowered himself onto a wicker rocker. Anna followed suit and Pratt wasted no time getting down to business. "Mr. Miller. Do you remember a story you wrote in July of 1964? It was a story that involved the mayor and a young girl who worked in his home."

Theodore Miller's round, red face lost its jolliness. The bird-like gaze sharpened. He stood up and moved toward the door. "I'm sorry. I have no idea what you're talking about. You should leave now."

They'd been prepared for his reaction. Anna pulled the photocopy they'd made of her news clipping from her purse and stood, handing it to the reporter. "This story has your byline on it."

He took the sheet and his face paled several shades. His eyes widened with horror. He looked at Anna. "Where'd you get this?"

"It was in a piece of furniture. But I can't find any other reference to the story. I really need your help, Mr. Miller. A friend of mine is in trouble because of that story."

Miller shoved the paper back toward Anna, barely waiting for her to grab it before he let go. He acted as if the sheet of paper was infused with a biological substance. "We're all going to have trouble if you don't burn that thing and forget you ever saw it." He started to go inside the house and then stopped, turning back to Anna. "Please, Miss Yesterday. Let this go. Let the ugly past lie. Digging it up will only cause pain for a lot of people."

Pratt joined Anna. "Sir, someone's trying to keep this quiet and they've taken something very important to Anna in the process. We need your help. Do you have any notes on the story? Or a copy of it?"

The man's round head shook emphatically from side to side. "No. And if I did, I wouldn't give them to you. It would only put you in danger and it wouldn't bring that poor girl back." He grabbed Anna's hand again, his grip bruising. "Please, let it go."

Miller slammed the door shut in their faces. Anna turned to Pratt. "Bring the girl back? Did he kill her too?"

Pratt took her hand. "He might as well have. Come on, I'll explain on the way home."

They were climbing into Pratt's car when the police cruiser drove past and parked in front of Glynus Stevens's house. Anna looked at Pratt and he slammed the car door shut again. "Come on."

As they approached the house, Glynus opened the front door. The uniformed cop standing on her porch pulled off his cap. "Miss Glynus Stevens?"

Glynus frowned, her gaze sliding past him to Pratt and Anna. "Yes?"

"I'm very sorry, ma'am."

Her hand flew to her mouth and Anna rushed forward, climbing the steps to wrap a supporting arm around the other woman.

The cop inclined his head to Anna before telling Glynus, "We found your grandfather. I'm afraid he's dead."

Glynus gasped, her intake of breath morphing to a horrified sob. Her knees buckled and it was all Anna could do to support her into the house. Pratt suddenly appeared at Glynus's other elbow and, between them they got her settled on the couch. She was sobbing so hard she could hardly draw a breath.

Anna kept her arm around the other woman, trying to soothe her.

The uniformed cop followed them inside and greeted Pratt. "It's good to see you again, sir."

"Officer Dresden. I wish it could be under better circumstances. What happened to Mr. Stevens?"

The officer glanced at Glynus, obviously uncomfortable with what he had to tell them. "I'm not sure this is the time..."

Glynus sniffed and looked up at Dresden. "Please? I'd like to know what happened to him."

The young officer worked his hat through his fingers. "We found him alongside the highway, in a ditch. I'm afraid it looks like he was the victim of foul play."

Anna's eyes widened. She glanced at Pratt and he looked grim. "Hit and run?" Pratt asked.

"No." Dresden looked at Glynus. "He was...strangled...with a necktie. It was still wrapped around his throat."

Glynus sobbed loudly and Officer Dresden looked like someone had stepped on his throat. "I'm sorry for your loss, Glynus. When you're feeling better, can you stop by the hospital and identify your grandfather's body?"

Hiccupping and mopping at her eyes, Glynus murmured agreement.

Pratt followed Bill Dresden out of the house. "This is just horrible," he told the cop.

Dresden nodded. "It's the first murder Crocker has had in years. Everybody's taking it pretty hard."

"Can you identify the tie?"

Dresden's face reddened.

"What is it?"

The young cop lowered his head, dropping his voice. "You have to keep this quiet."

Pratt nodded. "You have my word."

Dresden sighed. "It's red, white, and blue. Like a flag."

"Oh." The flyer hanging outside the antique store flashed through Pratt's mind. "Like a certain politician always wears?"

"Yeah. Just exactly like that."

"Well, crap."

"Yeah. Just exactly like that too." Dresden pointed a finger at Pratt. "Hey, I was gonna call you later. I got a bit distracted by all this… But that cop you were looking for, from the nineteen sixties?"

"Yeah?"

"I ran it by the Chief. He told me Crocker only had a Town Marshal and one cop in those days. They're both gone now, and I still need to do some digging on the cop, but it turns out that Chief Wilker's dad was the Town Marshal. Apparently, Marshal Wilker was good friends with Mayor Bethesda. The Chief told me their family had tons of stories about the two men spending time together, fishing, drinking too much at the local bar." Dresden shook his head, grinning. "Hard to believe Chief Wilker's related to the man he told me about. He's just about as strait-laced as a man can get without putting on the collar."

Pratt thought about Dresden's information. It was really bad news for him. The Chief would be the obvious person to ask for information about whether his dad was involved in a massive cover-up. And it was unlikely the Chief would be willing to believe his father was involved.

"Did I give you bad news?"

"You did." Pratt thought about it for a minute, wondering if he could or should share what he suspected with Officer Dresden. One thing that had made Pratt a good cop was his gut. He was a good judge of character and his instincts about people were usually pretty good. He had a good feeling about Officer Dresden, so he decided to go for it. "I have reason to believe the person I'm looking for colluded with then-Mayor Bethesda to cover up a crime. I doubt your Chief is going to accept that and I really need to get some first-hand information about what was going on at the time of the crime."

Dresden frowned. He stared at Pratt for a long moment, his wide hazel eyes looking stern. As silence stretched between them, Pratt was tempted to start talking again, to explain further, but Dresden finally gave a curt nod, saving him from babbling.

"I can see your problem. I tend to agree. But there might be another way if what you suspect is true. I'll need you to fill me in on what you have though."

"I'm not sure I can do that."

"You'll have to, if you want my help."

"This has been very sensitive, Officer…"

"Bill."

"Bill. Since we started looking into it, Anna's store has been broken into, we were attacked at the print plant…"

"Attacked? What were you doing there? Who attacked you?"

"Yes. I plead the fifth. And we don't know but I intend to find out."

Dresden's stern face slowly softened with a grin. "You plead the fifth, huh?"

Pratt didn't share his smile. "And Buck Stevens was murdered."

Dresden's smile faded. "You think Buck's death has something to do with your little problem?"

"I do."

Dresden expelled a breath, scrubbing a hand over his cheeks. "I need you to come down to the station and give me a statement."

"I can't."

"That wasn't a request, Mr. Davies."

"Pratt. And we can't do this by the book. If I'm right, this goes all the way to the mayor of Crocker. He has tentacles all over. And, correct me if I'm wrong, but I'm guessing that, since their dads were best buds, your Chief and the current mayor are pretty tight too. Am I right?"

Dresden twisted his lips in a grimace, looking away, across the street, where shoppers and bar hoppers were happily oblivious to the drama unfolding in the Stevens house. Finally, he sighed. "I'll come by Yesterday's later today. We can keep this off the books until I see what you have in the way of evidence. I can't promise that I won't go to the Chief once I see your evidence, but I can promise I'll listen to your case and take it into account in my decision."

Pratt wasn't entirely happy with Dresden's offer, but he realized Buck's murder had put everything into a new level of dangerous. He was no longer willing to operate entirely outside the purview of the Crocker PD. "Okay. I don't like it but, that's fair."

The door slammed shut behind them and Dresden touched the brim of his hat. "I'll see you later, Pratt."

Anna joined him on the sidewalk, looking grim. "What was that about?"

"I'll tell you in the car. We need to get back to the store. Dresden's coming over in a while." He jerked his head toward the house. "Is she gonna be okay?"

Anna blinked and looked down. A scraggly orange cat was twining around her legs, its mangled tail caressing her leg. She leaned down and petted it. "Well hello there, kitty. Where'd you come from?" The cat meowed and pressed its face into her hand. She glanced at Pratt. "I think she'll be all right. I offered to take her to the hospital but she declined. She just needs some time alone to adjust to the idea. She and her grandpa might not have been close, but it's a shock to learn that someone's gone, let alone murdered."

"Yeah. Murdered." Pratt frowned.

"Is that what you and Dresden were discussing?"

"That and other things. You ready?"

Anna gave the cat one last pat and started toward the car. Pratt opened the door for her and, before he could stop it, the cat jumped into the car ahead of Anna. "What the…"

She laughed as the stray climbed into her lap, purring. "Isn't that sweet?"

"Yeah, sweet." Pratt reached for it. "Come on buddy. You need to le…" The thing spat at him and swatted his hand, snagging him with a claw. "Ouch! Dangit!"

Anna pressed her lips together but he saw the laughter sparkling in her eyes. "I guess he's coming with us."

"What are you going to do with him?" Pratt could hear the thing purring from where he stood outside the car.

Anna touched noses with the cat. "I could use a mouse catcher in the store. He'd be purrrrfect." She grinned.

"Ha, ha. Very funny." Pratt pretended grumpiness but, as he closed the car door, he had to admit to himself that the stupid feline had put a smile on her face. Something he couldn't help being grateful for. If the cat could make her smile like that, Pratt would just have to put up with it.

CHAPTER FOURTEEN

The locksmith's father, Anton Friese, agreed to talk to them early the next day, before Anna opened the store. Once that was set up, Anna spent some of the time waiting for Dresden by prepping new items for sale in the store. Her new mouser lay on the worktable beside her, doing his best to create order out of the tangled, dirty mess of his striped, orange coat. Anna talked to him as she worked and discovered that he had very intelligent green eyes and he seemed to like hearing her voice. The more she talked to him the louder he purred.

The bell on the front door jangled as she was cleaning an old silver tea set. Pratt was shaking Dresden's hand when she emerged from the workroom. "Hello again Officer Dresden."

He pulled his hat off his head and offered her his hand. "Ma'am." The young officer looked around. "I've always wanted to come in here. My mom has a soft spot for antiques."

Anna nodded. "They tie us to the past in a way nothing else can." They shared a smile. "Can I get you something to drink? Something cold? Something hot?"

"Maybe just a water, if you have one."

She got him a bottle of water and they sat down at an old wicker set with a glass table. The cat wandered in and draped itself over a sunspot slanting across the floor near Anna's feet.

Dresden drank his water gratefully, nearly draining the bottle in one pull. "Thanks again, ma'am. That tastes wonderful."

"Please call me Anna. If I can call you Bill."

He nodded. "Now tell me what you've learned so far and let's figure out how I can help."

Anna handed Dresden the copy she'd made of the news article. "I'm sorry it's a copy. After everything that's happened, I'm reluctant to bring the original out of hiding. I'll show it to you if you really need to see it."

"No problem. I understand. But I'll need to see the original at some point." The young officer scanned the article, whistling softly. "If this is true..." He shook his head, leaving the thought dangling on the air between them.

"It's true. We just need to figure out how to prove it." Pratt filled Dresden in on Anna's early discovery of the article and her follow-up search. He also told the cop about Bethesda's subsequent visit to the store, the break-in, and their ill-fated visit to the printing plant.

"Any idea who might have locked you in the basement?"

Pratt shook his head. "None. And we didn't find anything at the plant. Though I'd like to go back and search that box of copy tubes. It's possible the original copy is stored down there."

"That would be an incredible long shot." Dresden told him. Glancing at Anna he asked, "Why didn't you report the break-in?"

"They didn't take anything. Besides, I know it's tied to the news article, and I wasn't ready to share that yet." Anna glanced at Pratt. "Despite what the mayor obviously thinks, I'm not anxious to stain his reputation. I just want to make sure there isn't a criminal running around."

"Or several," Pratt added.

Anna nodded. "If this thing actually happened and then was covered up, some poor woman was raped and god knows what else and she never got any justice. I'd like to give her that at least. Wherever she is."

"I don't think she cares anymore." Pratt turned at Anna's outraged gasp and hurried to explain. "I think she killed herself right after the rape."

"You didn't tell me that," she said angrily.

He gave her an apologetic look. "I know, I'm sorry. I'd intended to tell you tonight, but since Bill was coming over, I thought I'd just share my suspicions once."

"You're talking suicide?" Dresden frowned.

Pratt nodded, pulling a folded set of papers from his pocket. "I went back to the library this morning, after I stopped by the PD." He handed the papers to Anna. "I found these two stories. They happened a couple of months after the alleged rape. I think they're connected."

Anna glanced at the story of the woman who committed suicide and the one about the new dry goods store. Gilfers. "I remember these." She looked at Pratt. "I agree it's an incredible coincidence that Gilfers was in the news directly after, but it's no surprise that he opened the store. We already knew that." She handed the papers to Dresden.

"Yes, but the timing is just too much of a coincidence. And the girl hanging herself in her family's basement..." Pratt shook his head. "That article doesn't explain why she would have killed herself. They talk about general depression for a couple of months. Rape will do that to you. Especially if the rapist is someone of power who got away with it."

"But her name is different."

"Copper Smith." Dresden nodded, scanning the article.

"If you read through the story, you'll see the mother's name was Smith before she married. I'm guessing she and the girl used her name when the mother divorced old Mr. Gilfer."

Anna's eyes widened. "They were divorced?"

Pratt shrugged. "I'm just guessing, otherwise the girl would be Copper Gilfer. Besides, you met the old guy. Wouldn't you divorce him?"

Anna grinned. "You have a point."

"That's a lot of guessing, Pratt." Officer Dresden was apparently a "by the book" kind of guy and Pratt seemed to tend more toward an instinct and seat of the pants methodology.

"So how does the hardware store fit in?" Anna asked.

"Think of the chain of events. Mayor rapes girl. Girl kills herself. Father of girl suddenly comes into some money to buy himself a business."

"Follow the money." Dresden nodded.

Anna's stomach tightened at the inference. It was just too horrible. "Are you saying you think old Mr. Gilfer took a payoff to keep quiet when his daughter was raped?"

"That's what my gut is telling me. Now the trick will be to find out if it's true."

Dresden was shaking his head. "I can't believe all this could go on under the Town Marshal's nose. A small town is a hotbed of rumor and speculation."

"But you had one very powerful and motivated perpetrator, whose best friend was the town's head cop. If they managed to contain the circle of people who knew what happened, paid them off or got rid of them some other way, it could be contained."

"So, they would have had to deal with the girl, her father, the publisher and reporter at the paper, the owner and lithographer at the print plant…" Anna shook her head. "It seems like a pretty long list."

"Yet they did it." Pratt lifted his eyebrows. "Nobody breathed a word of this until you found that article.

She thought for a minute. Then she glanced at Pratt, "Mayor Bethesda thought I was blackmailing him. He said he'd gotten some phone calls."

Pratt nodded. "I'm guessing one of the players is in need of cash and desperate enough to go for it. Either that or somebody else found out about the rape."

"In addition to me?" She shook her head, skeptical.

"I agree," Dresden offered. "After keeping it contained all these years, it seems unlikely it would suddenly break loose in more than one place." Dresden shook his head. "I think your first idea is right. Bethesda had to know it was only a matter of time before one of the players decided he would use the gold mine at his fingertips."

"But all of these people are guilty too. They colluded with the mayor to cover everything up," Anna said.

Pratt nodded. "Which is why the mayor felt reasonably certain his secret was safe. Anyone who took a payoff and then kept quiet as that poor girl suffered and eventually killed herself was basically an accessory to her rape and worse."

Dresden frowned. "But Indiana's statute of limitations on rape, especially when it ends in death, can be unlimited, depending on the exact circumstances. Those people are still in danger of being prosecuted."

"They're fairly safe though, right? In order to point the finger at them, Mason would have to go public about what his father did. He's not going to do that right now. It might be the death knell for his candidacy."

"That's true, Pratt." Dresden shook his head. "What a mess." He thought about it for a minute and then nodded as if he'd made a decision. "Okay, what can I do to help?"

"I was really hoping you'd ask." Pratt leaned forward, resting his arms on his knees. "Anna and I are going to talk to someone who knew Gilfer during that time. Hopefully he'll be able to shine the light on some of that history. Since you have access to stuff I no longer do, can you check into the purchase of Gilfer's. See if you can trace the money back to anybody or anything?"

"You mean like an insurance policy? Or an unexplained deposit of a large sum of money?"

"Exactly."

"And can you check into the lithographer, what was his name…" Anna frowned thoughtfully, "Max…Max Smith. The printer at Quality said he thought the man was still alive and living at Happy Acres senior home."

"That should be easy enough to check." Dresden stood. "I'll talk to the Chief too…" He held up his hand when Pratt would have objected. "I'll be careful. I won't tell him what we suspect. But he might be able to tell me more about the Bethesdas and their relationship with the community around that time." He shrugged. "There might be something we can use to figure all this out."

Anna gave the man an impulsive hug. "Thank you so much for your help, Bill. It means a lot to me."

When the young liaison officer left, Anna succumbed to the sadness she'd been fighting since Joss disappeared. It felt like nothing they were doing would get Joss back. She drooped in her chair, fighting tears.

When Pratt came back from locking the door behind Dresden he crouched down beside her chair and touched her arm. "What's wrong, Anna?"

She sniffed, rubbing her arms under a sudden chill. She suspected Bess was nearby, in her own state of mourning. "I miss Joss. I can't believe we haven't heard from the thief yet."

Pratt's eyes widened slightly. "Oh, yeah. About that…"

The cat jumped into Anna's lap and gave her a nudge on the arm with its cold nose. She stroked it absently. "What? Did you hear something?"

***

Pratt scanned the clipping and pulled the memory stick he'd scanned it onto from the machine. He turned as Anna came into the room, carrying a very unhappy cat. "He keeps trying to go out the door with me."

Pratt looked around Anna's office, trying to think of a good hiding place for the stick. He spotted the freshly filled litter box in the corner and grinned. "That'll work."

Anna grimaced. "It would work for me. I'd never dig around in that thing looking for anything."

Pratt slid the stick beneath the plastic lining the pan. "*Au contraire*, you'll be digging around in here looking for gold by tomorrow. That's when the smell will drive you to action."

"Ha, ha." She swiped her hands down her jeans, obviously nervous about what they were about to do. "Are you sure we're doing the right thing?"

Pratt folded the newspaper and slipped it into a large plastic bag with a zippered top. "No. Not at all. But I don't think we have a choice."

"We're homing in on discovering what's going on, though. What if we give up our only evidence and then find out we needed it to arrest this guy?"

"Buck's murder put an end to our search for this guy, Anna. I'm not risking your safety to look for a murderer. Our best hope is to give him the paper and hope he assumes our part in this is done."

She placed her hands on her hips, her face darkening with anger. "What about Joss?"

Pratt touched her arm. "I didn't say we *were* giving up, only that I hoped the killer believed we were. I promised you we'd find your ghost and I meant it."

Her expression softened. "Thanks, Pratt. I'll owe you big time."

"You don't owe me anything. This jerk has stomped on my last nerve and I look forward to putting his ass behind bars."

"Okay. Let's get this done so we can get my friend back."

***

They parked in front of the River Barge Bar and climbed out of the car. Pratt looked at Anna. "I really wish you'd stay in the car."

"Nope. If this is dangerous then I'm going to be there to help. I'm not going to let you face it alone, Pratt."

"I'm trained for this sort of thing, Anna."

She shook her head stubbornly. "Let's go."

Sighing, Pratt started off around the building. His head swiveled as he scanned the area searching for movement. It turned out there was lots of movement. And noise. The River Barge Bar had a wide porch on the riverside that was filled with late-night revelers. To make things worse there were steps leading down to the grounds from the porch and a dirt path customers could follow down to a short dock, where it seemed popular sport to fling stuff into the river for the fish.

At least ten twenty-somethings were currently weaving and stumbling toward the end of the dock, shrieking with laughter as they nearly fell off.

"Seriously?" Pratt muttered. "Doesn't the owner of this bar have any sense of self-preservation?"

Anna shook her head. "God protects the stupid, I guess."

Pratt grabbed her hand. "Let's walk down here, behind the shops, where it's dark and quiet."

Pratt held onto Anna's hand because he wanted to make sure he could tug her down if bullets started flying. At least that's what he told himself. Actually, he held onto it because it felt small and velvety soft in his hand. And it kept her close enough so that he could enjoy her sweet, vanilla and peaches scent.

They stopped at a spot where the ground climbed high enough to make getting to a dock difficult. The water splashed against a rocky shore eight feet below them, leaving a dirty-looking foam behind as it retreated.

Pratt looked around, listening carefully. He didn't see anyone nearby or hear anything closer than the rowdies on the dock down the street. He glanced at Anna. "I think we're a go."

She nodded, shivering.

He pulled his leather jacket off and draped it around her shoulders.

She tugged it close. "Thanks."

"Okay, you stay here." Pratt walked over to the edge of the lawn and crouched down, easing himself over the edge and digging the toes of his boots into the uneven surface of the bluff to work his way down. As he stood in the narrow, sandy band at the base of the bluff, brown water splashing over his boots, he pulled the baggie from beneath his shirt, where he'd tucked it into the waistband of his jeans, and crouched down, holding it over the water.

A rock skittered down the bluff and he looked up, seeing Anna standing there. "Go on, Pratt. We have to do it."

The firmness in her voice impressed him. She had so much riding on that article. The loss of her friend, her business, and even her life were tied up in it. And, in the end, when he couldn't help wondering if they were doing the right thing, she was the one who let her convictions speak to them. She was as strong as she was beautiful. A truly incredible woman.

Pratt realized in that moment that he was falling in love with Anna Yesterday. And that opened up a whole new can of worms. He reached toward the water and settled the baggie onto its surface. The current grabbed it and sent it gliding downstream, moving it inexorably toward the center, where the water spun and roiled with violent energy.

He started to climb back up the bluff. The night sky shifted and the moon shone briefly through. Pratt saw a flash of something on the river. He stopped, crouched back down, and peered skyward. Light gray clouds enclosed the bright surface of the moon again but a clear patch of sky was nearby.

"What is it?" Anna asked.

Pratt shushed her softly. "Give me a minute," he whispered.

A moment later the clouds cleared again and Pratt saw the definite shape of a small boat, bobbing against the current on the opposite side of the river. Almost immediately the motor engaged and the boat started to move, following the bobbing speck of the plastic package down the river. He took off running, shouting to Anna as he ran. "Stay there!"

His feet splashed through the shallow water at the edge of the river, saturating the scuffed leather. The bottoms of his jeans quickly became soaked and he had to be careful not to trip over rocks and debris that had washed up against the bluff. The boat was ahead of him, moving steadily toward the package bobbing along on the current. He managed to keep it in sight, despite the bad visibility. The boat struggled against the chop and roll of the water and Pratt could only assume the driver had to work to avoid rocks and sand bars. He ran up against a rocky bluff that bulged out over the river and he had to stop and climb.

By the time he reached the top he had to run full out to catch up to the boat again. It was moving quickly up the river, heading for a bridge ahead. Pratt realized the driver must have picked up the clipping. He hit the bridge running hard and stopped, listening for the sound of the motor.

Silence.

He took off running again and emerged on the other side of the river just as a car shot away from the side of the road, throwing dust and gravel as it gunned the motor and tore down the road. Pratt tried to read the license plate but the car was moving too quickly and the back of the big, dark car was covered in rock dust and mud. "Dangit!"

Huffing and puffing from his sprint, Pratt bent over and placed his hands on his knees, trying to catch his breath. Once he could breathe again, he pulled out his cell and called Anna. Then he headed down to the river bank to find the discarded boat.

CHAPTER FIFTEEN

"A resident reported his fishing boat stolen this morning," Dresden told Pratt over the phone the next morning. "The hull identification number on the boat you found last night is a match."

Anna pointed to the street sign and Pratt took a right turn. "You're sure the guy reporting it wasn't our guy?"

"He's new in town. He and his family moved here from Tennessee just last year. It's highly unlikely."

"Okay. Thanks. We're pulling up at the Friese place right now. I'll call you later and fill you in if we learn anything interesting."

They parked in front of a square house covered in red brick. The concrete driveway was cracked, with weeds sneaking up through the fractures, but the yard and house seemed in good shape. A small, green car sat in front of the detached garage behind the house.

Anna put her hand on Pratt's arm as they started up the sidewalk. "Remember, I need to do most of the talking. Mr. Friese thinks I'm writing the history of Crocker."

Pratt put his arm around her waist, thinking she felt like she belonged there. "I promise I won't speak unless spoken to."

She laughed, shaking her head. "That'll be the day."

***

Anna knocked on the front door and glanced around. The brick beneath their feet was swept clear of debris and, on either side of the door, a large, clay pot held a bright assortment of daisies. A hummingbird feeder hung from a shepherd's hook not far from the entrance. It was obvious Mr. Friese enjoyed his home and yard and took good care of them.

She had a sudden wish for her own yard. Someday she'd do the whole house and yard thing. It would be really nice to have her own little piece of the world. Besides, Anna thought she might be a pretty good gardener given the chance.

The door opened and a man with gray hair and a tanned, wrinkled face stood looking at them. He smiled, showing them straight teeth that looked like they were his own. Anton Friese extended his hand. "Hello. You must be Anna?" The man had to be in his eighties, but he was tall, with a straight spine and long limbs that still looked strong and healthy. He even had a full head of steel-gray hair on his head.

She nodded. "I am. And this is my assistant, Pratt Davies."

Mr. Friese turned his wide smile on Pratt. "It's nice to meet you, Mr. Davies."

"Call me Pratt, please."

The man nodded, stepping back. "Come on in. I made coffee and forced myself to put some of my favorite muffins on a plate to share. I'm not generally very good at sharing. Especially with things I cherish." He laughed good-humoredly and Anna joined him.

"I'm exactly the same way. I tend to hide my favorites so nobody else can get to them."

"So that's why the chocolate keeps disappearing." Pratt narrowed his eyes on her. "I thought you were eating it all."

She grinned. "Not *all* of it. I hid some of it because you're almost as big a chocoholic as I am."

Friese led them through the house and out a sliding door to a patio. The glass-topped table was set with small plates and mugs, a silver-toned thermos sitting at its center, alongside a plate filled with muffins. "Please, sit."

Friese filled each of their mugs and offered the muffins.

Anna's eyes widened. "Are these gingerbread?"

He beamed. "Homemade. My mama's recipe."

She took a bite and moaned appreciatively. "Good heavens, that's good. I don't suppose you'd share the recipe?"

Friese laughed, settling into his own chair. "Young lady, you're lucky I shared the finished product."

She wiped her fingers on the napkin beside her plate and reached into her purse for her notebook. "I really appreciate your taking the time to talk to me today, Mr. Friese."

"My pleasure. Us old guys don't get a lot of visitors."

"You don't look much like an old guy," Pratt told him. "I hope I'm in half as good a shape as you when I'm your age."

"Thanks, son. I attribute it to good genes, clean living, and daily reps on the weight machine."

Pratt stuffed the last bite of his muffin in his mouth. "These muffins probably don't hurt."

Laughing, Friese agreed. "Food is a wonderful way to stay in touch with your past, don't you think, Anna?"

"Absolutely. In fact, I'm toying with the idea of having a food section in my book. Maybe I'll have a gingerbread muffin recipe to add to it." She lifted her eyebrows hopefully.

"If you do it won't be mine." His gray eyes sparkled with mischief and she had to laugh.

"Okay, I give up. We recently met your son, sir. He's a very nice man," Anna told him.

The older gentleman inclined his head in agreement. "I'm very proud of Scott. He's made a good life for himself. I just wish he'd get married and settle down. I could use some grandkids."

Anna covered her shock by looking at her pad. Scott Friese seemed a little old to be starting a family, but she guessed the old man had a dream. She knew from personal experience how hard it can be to let go of a dream once you've set your sights on it. "I'm sure he will someday."

"So, you're writing a book about Crocker?"

"I am. Yes. I'm interviewing some of the business owners in town, focusing on the ones who've been here the longest. That obviously puts Gilfers on my list. I spoke to Mr. Gilfer the other day—" She felt a little guilty inferring that the discussion had been about her book but she guessed technically it could have been. "—and now I'm talking to some of his acquaintances. So, I can get a well-rounded view of the man and the business. Scott told me you've known old Mr. Gilfer since grade school."

Friese nodded. "I have. We used to play together. I once considered us friends."

"Once?"

"I don't want to speak ill of the man. Let's just say we grew apart."

"Scott told me Mr. Gilfer turned bitter. Could that have been the stress of running his business? Starting a new business can be quite a shock. I know from personal experience."

"No. He suffered a personal tragedy and it turned him dark and hateful. I understand the pain of loss. We all suffer that at some time or other in our lives. But most of us find a way to go on with our lives. Gus didn't. He let it darken him. I've never seen an angrier man. I never could get him to talk about it, though I tried often enough. His wife had left him the year before and he was bitter about that too. She wouldn't let him see the kids…"

"Copper and Frank?"

Friese glanced at Pratt. "Yes. Copper's death was a tragedy. Poor thing. She committed suicide a few months before Gus opened Gilfer's. At least something good came from that poor girl's death." Friese shook his head.

Pratt frowned. "What do you mean, sir?"

Friese sipped his coffee. "It was the most wonderful thing." He pointed to Anna's notebook. "You'll want to write about this in your book. After Copper's death, Mayor Bethesda went to Gus and offered him the money to open his store." Friese shook his head. "The Bethesdas had…have…tons of money so it probably didn't even put a dent in their bank account, but to just give a man money like that, well, it was such a kind thing. It's why this town has always loved the Bethesdas. And why we're doing our damnedest to get young Mason elected into the United States Senate."

"Why do you think the mayor did it? Gave Gus the money?" Anna asked as she scribbled notes.

"Well, young Copper worked for the Bethesda family. She'd been a maid there since she turned sixteen. I know Mrs. Bethesda was very fond of the girl. In fact, Mrs. Bethesda left her husband not too long after Copper died. Speculation at the time was that grief tore them apart. Copper was only eighteen when she…died. I'm guessing the Bethesdas wanted to do something nice for her family."

Pratt and Anna shared a look. Pratt leaned forward, addressing Friese. "Did Gus tell you about the money?"

"No. Gus isn't one to share personal stuff. The Town Marshal let it be known around the town. He was good friends with Mayor Bethesda, the senior, back then. He made it clear that the Bethesdas weren't telling anyone because they didn't want anybody to think they'd done it for political reasons. But the Marshal wanted everybody to know what kind of mayor they had."

"I'll bet," Pratt murmured. Anna kicked him under the table.

"That's a wonderful piece of history, Mr. Friese. I hope you don't mind if I use it?"

"Not at all. I think it's time the Bethesda family got the credit they deserve."

"I couldn't agree more, sir. So, what about Frank? How did he take his sister's death, is he bitter too?" Anna asked.

"Frank was only ten years old when Copper died. From what I could see, he didn't really seem all that affected. Which is strange, but some siblings just aren't that close, I guess. And my initial perceptions could have been wrong. I didn't see Frank much after Copper's death. His mother took him away from Crocker after the divorce and he didn't return until years later, when he was an adult. He and Gus always seemed to have a good relationship and nothing Frank ever said or did gave me reason to believe he was bitter about what happened with his sister." Friese shrugged.

They talked about Gilfers for a while and then touched on a couple of the other older businesses in Crocker. Anna dutifully took notes and then, when she figured she'd gathered enough information to maintain her ruse of writing the book, she closed her notebook and stood. "Thank you so much for your time, Mr. Friese."

"It was my pleasure. I'm sorry you have to leave so soon. I hope you'll come back?"

Pratt shook the older man's hand. "We'd love to, sir. It was really nice chatting. You've been very helpful." Pratt reached for the muffins. "I hope you don't mind if I take a muffin for the road?"

Friese laughed, "Go ahead. I'm planning on making another batch later today."

Anna waggled her eyebrows. "What time? I might need to drop back to take more notes."

"Nice try, young lady."

***

Mason Bethesda sat at his desk, eating his usual lunch of salad and crusty Italian bread slathered with butter. He looked up when a knock sounded on his door. "Come."

His campaign manager walked in. "You wanted to see me?"

Bethesda sipped his water and wiped his mouth, pushing his salad away. "I wanted to get a report on the Yesterday matter. Did you send the IRS into her store?"

"I tried, but they couldn't get someone there for a couple of weeks. So, I went myself."

Mason dropped his napkin on top of the remains of his salad and looked up. "You what?"

"Don't worry. I wore a disguise. They didn't recognize me."

He sat back in his chair, amazed. "A disguise? Really? What, one of those fake noses with glasses attached. Holy crap, Reese! Are you really that stupid?" Bethesda stood up and started pacing the floor behind his desk. "Do I have to do everything myself?"

"I assure you, Mason, they didn't know who I was. My cousin is an actress and she made me up with a wig and stuff. I even borrowed a car from the city pool. It had an IRS-ish plate." He frowned, remembering how stupid he'd felt driving around in that car. It belonged to a woman in Records who'd been audited one too many times and had a serious grudge going on. "I made up a fake business card. It's all good."

Mason stopped pacing and sighed. "Well, it's done. I guess I'll just have to trust you on this one." He sat back down, scrubbing a hand over his face. "I'm a little jumpy after this morning's news."

"You mean about Buck Stevens?"

Mason watched his manager carefully, trying to judge his mindset about the news. "Yeah. Terrible thing. Buck and my dad were kind of friends."

Reese didn't say anything. He glanced toward the door. "If there's nothing else…"

Mason couldn't help himself. He had to know. "Who do you think killed him?"

Reese looked surprised by the question. "I...I have no idea. I never met the man."

"I know. It's just that, well, he was involved in that little problem I told you about. That concerns me a little." He let that sit for a minute before going on to add, "I'm a little worried some misguided fool is working his way through the players."

Reese's eyes widened. "You think you might be in danger?"

Mason shrugged. "Obviously I wasn't involved, but it's possible someone might decide to try to make me pay for something they perceive my father might have done."

"Seems far-fetched, Mason."

"To the rational mind, maybe. But we might not be dealing with a rational person. That's why I want the Yesterday woman dealt with. You're with me on that, right?"

Reese frowned. "I'm doing what I can, Mason."

"No, Reese. You're not. But I'm sure you can think of a way to do better." Mason sat down and picked up his phone, dismissing his manager. "Thanks, Reese. That will be all."

***

She stood in the center of the office and looked around. The room held its normal chill. There were no strange drafts or cold spots like before. The desktop was just as she'd left it. And she no longer had the sense that she wasn't alone in the room.

Sighing, Glynus pulled the first empty box close and opened it. Kneeling on the floor in front of the closet, she started going through the boxes of records her grandfather had kept there, looking for the information the potential buyers had asked for.

An hour later she straightened, looking around. She thought she'd found everything there was to find, but she wanted to be thorough, with her grandfather's death she realized she no longer wanted to run the print shop and she couldn't wait to get out of Crocker. She'd never felt quite at home there.

Her gaze fell on the safe. Sighing, she realized she'd have to take the cash to the bank. Her grandfather had always been the one to take it in, but obviously it would now be up to her. She crouched before the large, gray vault and dialed in the code. When it clicked, she turned the handle and pulled it open. Reaching inside, she pulled out the cash bags she'd placed there over the last couple of days. Her fingers bumped against something that felt like hard leather. Curious, Glynus reached back inside and grabbed it, pulling it out of the safe and examining it with a frown.

Why in the world did her gramps have an old, ratty looking gun belt and holster in his safe? Turning it over, Glynus saw a sticker on the underside of the gun belt. It read, "Property of Yesterday's Antiques".

The doorbell rang upstairs. Glynus shoved the money bags back in the safe and stood. On a whim, she brought the holster with her as she climbed the stairs to the main level. She'd do some digging to find out why her gramps might have had the tattered gun rig in his safe. Glynus opened the front door and found Heather Johnson standing on her doorstep, holding a casserole dish. Her son, Pierce stood on the step below her, looking grumpy.

"Heather, what a nice surprise."

"Hi, honey. I wanted to stop by and tell you how sorry I am about your grandpa. And to give you this." She held the glass dish out and Glynus took it. It was still warm from the oven. "I hope you like tuna casserole."

"Oh, that's so kind of you. Yes, I love tuna casserole. My mom used to make it for us kids all the time. Would you like to come in?"

"If I'm not bothering you." Her glance fell to the gun belt in Glynus's hand.

"Not at all. I was just cleaning some stuff out of my grandfather's office."

Heather turned to Pierce. "Come on, son. We're going to visit with Miss Glynus for a few minutes."

Pierce glared at his feet. "I don't want to come inside. You're being very inconsiderate, Mother. I'm supposed to be looking for the cowboy. I promised Miss Yesterday."

"Pierce!"

Glynus touched Heather's shoulder. "It's okay, Heather. This kind of thing isn't very fun for young men." She favored Pierce with a smile. Though he was in his late teens, his lack of worldly experience made him seem younger. "Pierce, look what I just found downstairs. Do you like cowboys? If I'm right about the age, this belonged to a real, live cowboy a couple of hundred years ago."

Glynus held the gun belt and holster over both of her palms so he could get a good look at it. Pierce's gaze lifted reluctantly. He skimmed it and his gaze danced quickly away, but it soon returned. He was obviously interested. "Come on inside and I'll get you a snack. You can get a good look at this while you eat."

Pierce shrugged, but he followed them into the house and let Glynus settle him at the kitchen table with some cookies and the gun belt.

Glynus brought Heather's snack into the living room, handing her a glass of iced tea.

"Thank you, dear. You're so good with him."

Glynus shrugged. "My brother is autistic. I was several years older than him and the only one my parents felt comfortable leaving him with when we were growing up. I got lots of practice."

Heather sipped her drink. "He can be a challenge but he's a very sweet boy."

"Just like my brother." Glynus smiled. The doorbell rang again and Glynus went to the door to accept more casseroles and well-meaning Crockerites. Within the hour her little house was filled to the brim with people. There was so much noise and activity they didn't notice for another half hour that Pierce was gone. And so was the gun belt.

CHAPTER SIXTEEN

Pratt dropped Anna at the store and went to talk to Dresden about what they'd learned. Anna suspected he was hoping to get a look at the PD's computer records himself. They still needed something concrete to tie the first Mayor Bethesda to the crime outlined in the news story.

She opened the store and stopped just inside the door. It seemed so cold and empty without Joss. Tears filled Anna's eyes and she had to force herself to move inside and close the door.

Her new business partner greeted her with a soft, mewling sound, winding himself around her legs. "Hello. I need to come up with a name for you, don't I?" She reached down and scratched the big cat's bony back. He was a little tidier than the last time she'd seen him, but he still needed to put on some weight. "I'll call you Bones, since that's about all you've got left. Bones and fur. Let's go get you some more tuna." She made a mental note to buy cat food the next time she was out. She'd had a bag of cat litter in her workshop for cleaning up paint spills, so she'd been able to give him a litter box at least. But a cat could not live on tuna and half and half alone. Though he might wish he could.

Bones followed her to the small kitchenette area and accepted his tuna gratefully. She gave him fresh water and then washed her hands. The front doorbell jangled as she was drying them. She was amazed to find Tatty Baker and his mother standing just inside the door, looking around, when she exited her workroom. Anna hurried toward them, offering the old woman her hand. "What a nice surprise, Mrs. Baker. How are you today?"

Mrs. Baker pinched her lips, her shaggy, white eyebrows lowering. "I come to get my property back from you, girl."

Anna's mouth opened and she glanced at Tatty, unsure how to respond.

Tatty smiled. "Sorry, she's a bit worked up…"

"Shut up, boy."

He ignored her. "She's had a moment of clarity and remembers seeing the news clipping you mentioned the other day. She's determined to get it back. If you'll just give it to her, we'll get out of your hair."

The wiry black man continued to smile, but his brown eyes darted nervously around the store. It was clear he wasn't comfortable with their errand.

"I'm so sorry. I…I don't have it anymore."

"Where is it?" The old lady took a step forward, one shaky hand shooting out to grab Anna's arm. "I know you have it, girl. You told me."

The gnarled, brown fingers dug painfully into her forearm. Anna tried not to panic. She reached out and gently tried to remove the old woman's hand. "I gave it to someone already."

"Who?" Tatty appeared worried by the news.

Anna shook her head. "I'm sorry, I can't tell you."

Tatty looked down at his mother. "Mama, why don't you just look around the store for a couple of minutes, Miss Yesterday and me is gonna have a conversation."

Anna frowned, "Mr. Baker, I really can't tell you who has the clipping."

He nodded, taking Anna's elbow and leading her gently but firmly away from his mother. When they reached the back of the store Anna pulled her arm away and rounded the counter, putting it between them. "What did you want to talk to me about?" She let him know with her tone that she wasn't pleased about his pushiness.

"Look, Miss Yesterday. I wasn't completely honest with you when you came by the house the other day."

"Really?" She didn't even bother to try to hide her sarcasm.

Tatty sighed, dropping down onto the stool on the customer side of the counter. "I do remember the news article you were talking about. In fact..." He glanced across the store to make sure his mother was still out of earshot. "I found that article, pulled it out of the fire myself, almost fifty years ago."

"Oh, my Lord! I can't believe it. Why didn't you tell me?"

He lifted an eyebrow. "Ma'am, I'm sure you understand why. I'm just a simple man, trying to make an honest living. I don't need no trouble from the likes of Mason Bethesda."

She blew out a breath. "Join the club. Ever since I started asking questions about this story he's been all over me. I think he even sicced the IRS on me."

Tatty shook his head. "Look, to tell ya the honest truth, I done forgot about that paper. Mama did too. She liked to read so I give it to her. I don't know what she did with it after that. Knowin' her she just tucked it away." He shook his grizzled, salt and pepper head. "I was only ten but I knew them men in the field was doing somethin' they shouldn't."

"What men? What exactly did you see?"

"Two men burnin' a pile of papers in the center of the mayor's cornfield."

"Did you recognize them?"

Tatty shrugged. "No ma'am, I didn't know many adults in those days. We pretty much kept to ourselves."

"Can you describe the men to me?"

"My memory's not that good, ma'am. I just 'member one was tall and dressed like a dandy and th'uther was smallish and right messy. He had black smudges all over his clothes."

"Like a lithographer, maybe?"

He shrugged again and Anna suspected he didn't know what a lithographer was.

"Those are the men who worked at the printing plant, printing the papers."

"Could be, sure enough."

"Did you ever tell anybody what you saw?"

"Next day. I told Mama. She boxed my ears good and made me promise never to say another word about it."

"I can certainly understand that."

He nodded thoughtfully. "Them wasn't the best times for a po' black family, but we did okay. We was happy and nobody much bothered us. Mama didn't want that to change."

"So why did she keep the paper?"

"Tell ya the truth I think she meant to throw it out but the old man grabbed it up with a bunch of other stuff one day, meanin' to burn it in the fireplace, and she 'bout had a kitten and four pups." He laughed, shaking his head. "She used every bit of everything we had until it was just about in tatters. She's built that way. Real frugal."

Anna frowned. "When I came to the house the other day, she lied to me about the news clipping."

"No, I don't think she did. But old Gus, he had some suspicions about it and he give her a hard time. In fact, he wouldn't let up on her 'til I fessed up and he had seven kinds of conniption fits." Tatty scrubbed an age-speckled hand over his mouth, glancing sideways again. "She's a lot frailer than she seems, ma'am. It's my job to protect her. I thought I'd come here today and beg you to give me that paper back. Old Gus won't let us be 'til you do."

"I wasn't lying, Tatty. I can't give it to you. I don't have it anymore. Somebody broke into the store and stole something very precious to me and the only way I could get it back was to give them the paper. Pratt and I delivered it last night."

"Who'd you give it to?"

"I don't know. We were told to drop it and somebody picked it up."

Tatty frowned. "This is bad, ma'am. Very bad."

"We're working hard to find the person responsible for all of this. We're getting very close."

"You get the paper, boy?" Coming from the other side of the shop, the old woman's voice throbbed with impatience.

Tatty held Anna's gaze as he reached for the newspaper on the countertop, pulling a sheet off the top. "Yes, ma'am. I got it right here." He folded the sheet of newsprint, stuffing it into the front of his shirt. "We can go now, ma'am." He inclined his chin to Anna and turned away, shuffling across the store to gather up his mother.

Anna bit her lip as she watched them leave, feeling terrible. She hoped Tatty could hold old Mr. Gilfer off until they could prove his part in the current mess. Then maybe they could get Gilfer to leave the Bakers alone.

***

The front door opened and Anna looked up from her inventory book. She was surprised to see Pierce Johnson standing there. He was wearing rubber dish-washing gloves and holding Joss's gun belt. She gave a little shriek and ran around the counter, heading for the boy.

He jerked, his eyes widening with alarm and glanced at the door as if considering making a run for it.

Anna quickly checked herself. "Hey, Pierce. What do you have there?"

"This belongs to the cowboy. He lives here and he's a cowboy. This holster belongs to a cowboy and it has Yesterday's Antiques written on it. It must be his. It would look funny on you, Miss Yesterday and that other man isn't even a cowboy." Pierce frowned, obviously angry with Pratt for not being a cowboy.

Anna clasped her hands together to keep from grabbing it out of the boy's hands. "Where did you find that?"

"Miss Glynus had it. Mother and I went there to give her food and cry. I don't like to cry so Miss Glynus showed me the cowboy belt and let me look at it while I ate cookies. She has good cookies. They were oatmeal but they didn't have disgusting raisins in them. I hate raisins. Why do they always put raisins in oatmeal cookies, Miss Yesterday?"

Anna barely heard him. Her gaze was locked on the belt. "Um…I don't know Pierce. Does your mother know where you are?"

Pierce frowned, his hands tightening on the cherished antique. "Miss Yesterday, I'm seventeen years old, I don't always need to be with my mother."

"No. Of course not. I just don't want your mother to worry." Anna looked around the store. Joss should have popped up. Where was he? Maybe she needed to touch the belt again. "Pierce, can I see that, please?" She tried to keep the emotion out of her voice but it shook a little none-the-less. "I think I can make the cowboy come if I hold it."

"Meow!"

Pierce blinked. "You have a decrepit looking feline. I've seen that feline before. He was outside Miss Glynus's house. He was spitting at one of the basement windows when I was looking for the cowboy."

Anna took a deep breath, blinking back tears as the cat wound around her legs, purring loudly. "Would you like to keep him company for a while, Pierce? I need to make a phone call."

The boy nodded. "I can do that. I'm sorry I got angry about my mother. She crowds me. I saw it on Dr. Phil once. A woman said her mother invaded her space and it reminded me of my mother. When she crowds me, it makes me angry. I'm my own man, Miss Yesterday."

"You certainly are. And thank you for bringing me Joss's gun belt. I'm sure he'll thank you himself when he comes back." She held out her hand, silently praying she wouldn't have to wrestle the boy for it. As he hesitated, glancing toward the door, Anna wondered if she'd be able to let him leave with his treasure. She was very much afraid she'd tackle him to the floor to get it back. But after another minute's hesitation, Pierce handed it over."

Anna clutched the belt and holster to her chest, closing her eyes. She could almost smell Joss, feel his warmth, hear his husky voice…

"Miss Yesterday, your cat is acting funny."

She opened her eyes. Bones was rolling around on the floor, smacking the air with his paws and spitting. His green eyes were wide, almost bulging. She watched him for a minute and he seemed to calm down. "He's all right. He just likes to play."

Anna carried the belt and holster to her office and locked it in the safe. Then she sat down at her desk and called Pratt. Her hand was shaking with emotion as she dialed. She got his voice mail so she quickly left him a message about the gun belt.

She sat there for another minute, trying to figure out how Glynus Stevens would have gotten Joss's gun belt. Was she the blackmailer? It would explain why the mayor assumed Anna was the guilty party. Especially after she showed up with the paper.

"Miss Yesterday?"

She looked up, realizing she'd zoned out with her thoughts. "What is it, Pierce?"

"There's a man here. He says he needs to talk to you."

She hurried into the store and stopped, her heart pounding hard in her chest. "What are you doing here?"

***

"We got the initial forensics back on Buck Stevens."

Pratt blew on the boiling hot coffee Dresden had just handed him. "Oh really? That was fast."

The other man chuckled. "Lucky for us we have a student in the Forensic Science program at Indiana

University working at the hospital. She's really smart and very excited about the field. She doesn't get a lot of opportunities to try out her knowledge around here so when a potential murder victim came into the morgue, she jumped right on it."

Pratt sipped the coffee, grimacing. "Gack. You should have your eager beaver forensics student test this coffee for arsenic."

Dresden shook his head. "Budget cuts. They make the coffee as foul as possible so we don't drink as much."

"So what did she find? I assume she verified that it was murder."

"She did, death by strangulation. She learned something else interesting. Apparently, Buck Stevens had several tiny cuts on the knuckles of one hand."

Pratt frowned. "Defensive wounds?"

"Unlikely. Too small. And she found minute traces of glass in the cuts."

Pratt sat up straighter. "Consistent with somebody who might have broken a window and reached through to unlock a door?"

"Yeah. That's what it looks like."

"Then Buck was the one who broke into the antique store."

"It appears that way. But just to be thorough I want to verify that he hasn't had to replace glass in his own home or car recently."

"You do that, but it'll be a waste of time. Buck was the thief. It makes perfect sense that he'd be involved. Quality printed the newspaper article Anna found. If there was a cover-up, Buck would have had to be involved."

"Why would he go along though? I looked into the bank records of all the involved parties and there was no record of Buck ever receiving a large sum of money from the mayor. Or anybody else for that matter."

"Remember what Anna told us about the history of Quality Print? How suddenly a business that was struggling to survive could do no wrong? Employees saying Buck had a golden touch? It's obvious the mayor paid Stevens off with business rather than cash. He just made sure all of his connections used Quality for their print business. That kind of payoff is a heck of a lot harder to trace."

Dresden thought about this. "I'll bet the publisher of the *Crocker Sun* was offered a similar deal. Maybe Quality printed the paper for cheaper than he could have gotten it printed elsewhere."

"It's worth checking into. The only question is, if Buck stole the gun belt, it would seem he was our blackmailer. But if that's true, then who killed *him*? Pratt asked.

"Gunbelt? I thought you and Miss Yesterday told me nothing was taken."

Too late, Pratt realized he'd given Dresden more information than he'd intended to. He grimaced. "Oh. Yeah, about that..."

***

Anna couldn't believe the IRaSs was back. Except, he looked different from before. She realized after a moment that his hair was shorter. And lighter. "My assistant told you we'd call to set up an appointment in your office for the audit."

The man pulled his dark sunglasses off and glanced at Pierce, who was sitting on the floor whipping a rubber dish glove around for Bones to chase. "Do you think we could talk in private somewhere?"

Anna frowned. The last thing she wanted was to be in a room alone with the man standing a few feet away from her. "No. Whatever you want to talk about can be discussed here."

He glanced at Pierce again and then nodded. "Can we at least walk over there?" He indicated the counter, "I have a responsibility to my employer to keep what I'm about to tell you confidential."

Anna didn't see any harm in that. "Okay." When she had the counter safely between her and the IRaSs, she crossed her arms over her chest and lifted an eyebrow, waiting for him to tell her why he was there.

"First of all, I'm not really with the IRS."

Anna's glare disappeared behind a look of shock. "Why did you say you were? You scared the crap out of me."

"I'm sorry about that. My boss made me do it, but I've been feeling guilty about it and, well, things seem to be escalating and I don't want any part of it."

"What do you mean?"

He sighed, settling his dark sunglasses onto the counter as he seemed to be thinking about how to start. "Look. I could lose my job over this so I'm asking you to keep what I'm about to tell you quiet. I know I don't deserve your consideration after scaring you…but I'm asking anyway. I'm ambitious, I'll admit that, but I'm not a thug. Though I'm starting to feel like one."

"Okay, you have my word that I'll listen with an open mind. That's all I can promise."

He nodded. "That's fair." He looked her in the eye. "My name is Perry Reese. I'm Mason Bethesda's campaign manager."

Her mouth came open. "Crap."

"Yeah. If he knew I was here I'd be fired on the spot. I'm not even sure I care. But here's the deal. Mason's determined to scare you away from this story. I think he wants me to do whatever it takes. I'm not willing to do that. The IRS thing was the best I could do. I just wanted to warn you that somebody is blackmailing him over the story. Which means two things. One, Mason is very jumpy and becoming desperate. And two, whoever the blackmailer is, he's dangerous. When I heard Buck Stevens had been killed, I realized Mason wasn't the only one who will apparently do anything to keep the story quiet. I…" He looked over his shoulder toward the door. "I think you're in danger, Miss Yesterday. Real danger."

She blinked, her heart rate picking up and her stomach twisting with fear. She'd known the Buck thing was bad, but she'd been so busy trying to figure things out that she hadn't given much thought to how it all affected her. Besides, once she gave the blackmailer the story, she figured he'd turn away from her. At that moment she realized she'd been naïve. She might not have the physical news clipping, but she still had knowledge of the event. That had apparently been enough to get Buck killed. "Why do you think Buck's death is related to this?"

Reese sank onto the tall stool, his attractive face dark with worry. "Buck came to me just before he disappeared. He assumed I knew what was going on and told me more than he should have about the...story...you have in your possession. He said he was afraid of what was going to happen and wanted me to help him with Mason. I couldn't believe such a story existed. It seemed preposterous such a thing could be hidden all these years. I told him to take a hike and to keep his mouth shut. Next I heard of him he was dead." Reese shuddered. "It's probably my fault he's dead. I should have done something."

Anna felt bad for the young man, who seemed to have gotten caught in the middle of a bad situation just as she had. "You couldn't have known. I'm still finding it all hard to believe and I've seen the story with my own eyes."

He nodded. "I couldn't live with myself if you got hurt too because I kept my mouth closed. And...to be honest...I don't know what Mason will do next. Even if I don't do what he wants, he's fully capable of finding someone else who will."

"You think Mason is behind Buck's death?"

"Oh no. Well, not really. But I've known him for a long time and Mason pretty much expects to get what he wants. If he doesn't...well...let's just say things get pretty ugly for whoever is standing in his way. The thing about Mason though is that he keeps a very low profile. He's like the wife beater who only punches his wife where the bruises won't show. Tying one of his ties around Buck's throat and leaving him out in the open is definitely not Mason's style."

When Reese left a few minutes later, Anna sat for a moment, thinking. She shivered, feeling a chill that hadn't been there before Reese arrived. She suspected Bess was nearby, though the specter hadn't shown herself much since Joss disappeared. She was obviously very upset and Anna couldn't do much to console her. Anna frowned at the thought. That was another concern for her. She couldn't figure out why Joss hadn't shown up once his gun belt was returned.

It suddenly occurred to her that he might be trapped at Glynus Stevens's house. She thought about that for another minute and then grabbed her purse. "Pierce, I need to go to Miss Glynus's house. Why don't you walk with me? I'm sure your mother is worried about you."

The boy climbed to his feet and walked to the door with her. "It's time for my lunch anyway. Mother will need time to prepare it properly."

Anna locked the door, amused when the cat pawed at the glass and meowed. "We'll be back soon, Bones."

Watching the cat pace and spit with anger at being left behind, Pierce frowned. "He has human eyes, Miss Yesterday."

Anna nodded. "I know exactly what you mean, Pierce. Sometimes I could swear he knows what I'm saying when I talk to him."

They walked in silence for a few minutes. The sun was high and hot in the sky, beating relentlessly down on their heads as they walked toward the Stevens home. The streets were busy, full of an early lunch crowd as well as people visiting the wide variety of shops in the picturesque town. With her mind spinning around everything going on in her life, Anna felt removed from it all. The streets and people of Crocker usually charmed her. But in that moment, she viewed them through a taint of unease. Any of the people she passed on the street could be their killer. The thought made her jumpy and she briefly considered trying to reach Pratt again. She'd feel better if he were with her.

They were only a block away from Glynus's house when Pierce stopped and made a strange sound, pulling her from her thoughts. Anna glanced at him. "What is it, Pierce? What's wrong?"

"That's the man I wanted to tell the cowboy about. He's a bad man. He talked about stealing something from Yesterday's Antiques. He didn't think I heard. Lots of people don't think I hear just because I'm special. I was going to tell the cowboy what the man said, but I never got a chance."

Anna followed Pierce's line of sight, frowning. Glynus Stevens was standing in her door, talking to a man Anna recognized. She sucked in a surprised breath.

Suddenly the pieces all clicked together.

***

"You're telling me Anna believes in ghosts?" Dresden's eyebrows lifted into his hairline.

"She does, and I do too so don't say anything that will alienate me as a friend. I've grown kind of fond of you."

Dresden thought about this for a minute and then grinned. "Okay, I won't tell you that I think you're nuts because I like you too."

Pratt chuckled. "Hey, did you ever check into that lithographer Anna found? Max…?"

"Max Smith, at Happy Acres." Dresden nodded. "That's a dead end. He died a few months ago."

"Well it was worth a try. Tell me what else your forensics genius found with Buck."

Dresden looked confused at the change of subject, then shook his head as if clearing his mind. "Oh yeah, this one is strange. Between you and me I think it's a never mind. The guy probably just had salad for lunch."

Pratt frowned, "Okay."

"Vinegar."

"What?"

"There was vinegar residue on the tie used to strangle Buck. Not on the end, like you'd expect from someone dribbling when he ate, but right on the part of the tie the killer gripped to kill him."

Pratt thought about that for a minute. There was something niggling at him. Something having to do with vinegar. What was it? He knew it was tied to one of the players of the current mystery, but he couldn't quite grasp the memory.

Then it clicked.

His eyes widened as the memory returned in a clarifying rush. "Holy crap! I know who killed Buck." He leaped to his feet, dialing Anna as he started for the door. He had to warn her.

"Wait, you have to tell me. Who is it?" Dresden grabbed his jacket and gun off his desk as he ran after Pratt.

Pratt was already rushing through the door. "I'll tell you on the way into town."

CHAPTER SEVENTEEN

Anna's first instinct was to take Pierce and run. But then she realized the man standing at Glynus Stevens's door might hurt the young woman. Even if Glynus were involved in everything that was going on, Anna couldn't just let her be hurt…or worse. And Heather Johnson might still be in the house. Anna turned to Pierce. "Listen to me, Pierce, you're right. That man is dangerous. I'm going to go over there and try to keep him from hurting anybody. I need you to go to the police department and get Pratt and Officer Dresden. Tell them to come here as quickly as they can. Can you do that for me?"

The boy frowned. "My mother might be in that house. The man could hurt her."

"I'm going to make sure that doesn't happen. Will you run to the police as fast as you can and tell them to come to Miss Stevens's house? Tell them I need their help."

Pierce nodded, turned, and hurried off down the street. "Be careful, remember the street rules," she called out to him. Anna frowned after the boy, worried, but she had to hope he would stay safe, and do as she'd asked. For all she knew, her safety and the safety of everybody in that house were at stake.

Taking a deep breath, Anna started across the street.

***

Pratt looked at his phone as Dresden drove and saw that he had two messages. He listened to the first one, which was from Theodore Miller. The reporter sounded frazzled, breathless.

Hello, Mr. Davies. This is Theodore Miller. I wanted to tell you that I've decided to share what I know with you. I don't have my original notes but I can tell you where they are, along with the marked-up copy from the story. Come to my house as soon as you can. I...I've got to go now, someone's at my door. Why couldn't you and the girl leave things be?

Pratt disconnected and thought quickly. The evidence Theodore Miller could give them would go far to prove that the story Anna had found really occurred. It would also shine the light on the fact that Mason Bethesda was at the center of a mess that included blackmail, harassment, and probably murder.

Pratt realized he needed to be in two places at once. They had to pick up the suspect in Buck's murder *and* collect the physical evidence that would cement the whole big mess. Since he had no reason to think the suspect knew he was on to him, Pratt decided the evidence had to take precedence. Having made his decision, Pratt looked at Dresden. "I think we've caught a break. The reporter who wrote the original story left me a message. He has actual physical proof of the story. He wants us to come by his house."

Dresden nodded. "Outstanding. Where?"

Pratt gave him directions as he accessed the second message. It was from Anna. He listened as Anna explained that Pierce had walked into the store with Joss's gun belt and that he'd found it at Glynus Stevens's house. Pratt frowned. What would Glynus have been doing with that belt? Luckily, they'd be just down the street from there and he could drop in to talk to the woman about it.

He punched in Anna's number to tell her he'd look into it. It rang several times before he gave up and disconnected.

***

Anna smiled at Glynus when she opened the door. The other woman looked tired and a little surprised to see her, but not scared. She hoped that meant she wasn't being threatened. Not yet anyway. "Anna, what a surprise."

Anna smiled, taking a step forward so Glynus had no choice but to step back and let her in. "I just came by to see how you're holding up. Are you okay?" Anna's gaze held the other woman's, with more intensity than the simple question implied. She was looking for any signs of duress in Glynus's gaze.

"She's just fine, Miss Yesterday."

Anna's head shot up and her gaze flew to the familiar face. "Hello, Frank. I didn't know you'd be here."

His smile turned cold. "Didn't you now? Funny, I thought you saw me come in. You were with that autistic boy, weren't you?"

Frank Gilfer reached behind his back and Anna reacted without thinking, pulling Glynus behind her and shoving her toward the door. "Run!"

But the gun came up and a bullet pinged off the door just to the side of Glynus's head. The woman screamed and Anna ducked with a shriek.

"I don't think anybody's going anywhere, Anna. Not until I find what I'm looking for here."

***

Dresden touched the front door and it swung inward. He motioned for Pratt to stand aside and pulled his revolver, turning sideways. "Mr. Miller, Crocker PD. Are you here?"

There was no response. Pratt caught Dresden's eye and the other man nodded. Pratt reached out and shoved the door inward, Dresden went in low. When no shots were fired, Pratt followed him inside.

The man's living room was trashed. Furniture lay on its side, framed pictures lay broken on the floor, and glass crunched under their feet. The legs of a small, marble-topped side table had been shattered into pieces and there was blood all over the round top.

Behind the overturned couch, Theodore Miller was stretched out, bleeding profusely from a wound on his head. Pratt hurried over as Dresden checked out the rest of the small house. The elderly man's pulse was weak.

"All clear," Dresden said when he returned.

Pratt looked up. "Call for an ambulance. He's still alive, but barely."

Before Dresden could dial 911 his cell rang. He looked at the display. "It's dispatch." He hit the call button. "Hey Gene. What? When? Okay, thanks. We'll go now. I'll need backup, and an ambulance dispatched to 9134 Jackson Street. Elderly man, eighties, he's unconscious and bleeding from a head wound."

He hung up and started for the door. "Pierce Johnson just showed up at the PD. He claims Anna Yesterday sent him to get you. She's at Glynus Stevens's house."

Pratt frowned. "Why would she send Pierce to the police department? Is Glynus okay?"

"I'm not sure. The dispatcher said Pierce was babbling something about a bad man hurting his mother."

Pratt stood and started for the door. "Gilfer must be there. Those women are in danger."

***

Anna straightened, holding her hands out in front of her. "Take it easy, Frank. Nobody is trying to stop you. You can just get whatever you came here for and leave. Nobody else needs to get hurt."

The man laughed, shaking his head. "It's all so f'd up. I was just gonna try to squeeze a little money out of that jerk.

But then you had to find that stupid news clipping. What were the chances of that happening?" Frank Gilfer's face was nearly purple with rage. "You messed up everything. I should kill you just because you screwed up my life. And then I should kill that evil old woman for leaving the paper in that dresser."

Anna put a hand on the small chair next to her, intending to dive behind it if Frank seemed like he was going to use the gun. "Now don't get crazy on us, Frank. It was just a fluke. But it isn't important now. Why don't you just go on and leave? Glynus and I won't try to stop you."

He snorted, sending snot shooting from his nose. He dragged a shaky hand across his face, his eyes bulging with panic. Anna's heart sank. The man was perched on the edge of insanity. He'd go over in the beat of a heart. "Just leave? And then what, you bitch? Go back to the hardware store and pretend nothing happened. After I killed Buck and that reporter? I don't think so."

Anna thought maybe she could distract him. "But you have the news clipping, right?" She hoped she was guessing correctly on that one. "You can give it to Mason and maybe he'll agree to help you work it out with the police in exchange for you not blackmailing him." It was a ludicrous idea of course, Mason would be more likely to make sure the man spent the rest of his life behind bars just because Gilfer had tainted his good name, but Frank was obviously not thinking clearly. Maybe he'd fall for it.

He swore. "The Bethesdas have gotten away with murder already. I'm not letting Mason walk from this. Copper was so darn young." He scrubbed a hand angrily over his face. "Nobody even tried to help her when she was suffering and in pain. Nobody cared until she killed herself. Then the only thing anybody seemed to care about was money and reputations. I'll never forgive my old man for his part in this mess. I'm going to make sure he goes to prison with Mason Bethesda."

Anna frowned. "But if you want the story to come out, why did you stop me?"

"Because I don't have what I need yet. As soon as the story breaks, I lose my leverage. This story will come out, but not until I want it to. Once I take care of you bitches, I'm going to pay Mason Bethesda a little visit to get as much money from him as I can. Then I'm getting the hell out of Crocker before launching the story to the world."

"What about Gramps?"

Anna turned to Glynus. The other woman had been so quiet Anna'd forgotten she was in the room.

"Why did you kill my grandpa?" Her face crumpled and she started crying. In that moment she looked like a small girl whose heart was breaking.

Ignoring Glynus, Frank went on talking to Anna. "The old monster told me what really happened to Copper. I'd known the old man was a cold fish, but I had no idea he was the devil. He apparently thought my forgiveness would win him a spot in heaven or something. Sick bastard. I told Buck what I planned but promised him if he helped me get that newspaper from you I'd make sure he stayed out of it. But then he figured out what the story was about and panicked. He knew at that point that he wouldn't be spared." Frank sniffed, his hand with the gun drooping lower as he talked. "The other night I caught him coming out of Bethesda's mansion. I knew then I couldn't trust him."

"So, you used a tie like Mason's to kill him, trying to lay the blame for Buck's death on Mason's doorstep."

Frank nodded. The gun drooped lower. Anna watched it carefully, looking for her chance. "That was pure genius if I do say so myself. That story about his dad raping my sister would only damage his reputation—"

Glynus gasped, her hand flying to cover her mouth.

"—but a murder charge would put him behind bars where he belongs."

Anna restrained herself from pointing out the hypocrisy of that statement. The only person in the current mess who was killing people was the guy holding the gun on her and Glynus. A shadow passed over the window behind Frank. Anna's eyes widened and Frank noticed, he started to turn.

"What are you looking for?" Glynus spoke up. She slid a look toward Anna before taking a step toward Frank to draw his attention. "Why did you come here? I hope you don't think I knew anything about this."

Frank shook his head. "I'm done talking to you two." He cast his gaze around the room, his hand shaking even harder. He lowered the gun to his side and Anna slid her gaze to Glynus, jerking her head toward the area behind the couch. Glynus nodded.

Frank's gaze landed on the long piece of furniture. He swung the gun toward Anna. "You, sit down there, and you…" he indicated Glynus, "Get me some heavy tape. Don't try anything or I'll kill her and come after you."

Anna's hand slid over the armchair. Her fingers grasped a small blanket folded over its back. Behind them, the sound of a shoe scuffing against the porch on the other side of the door told Anna help had arrived. She grabbed the blanket and yelled, "Now!"

Glynus threw herself sideways, behind the couch, as Anna flung the blanket toward Frank's face. The door exploded inward and Frank's gun went off, followed shortly by a second shot. Anna hit the floor hard, landing on Glynus's sneaker with a grunt of pain.

Shouting and screaming filled the small space and Pratt yelled for them to stay down. A moment later he came around the couch and grabbed her hand, pulling her off the floor. "Are you all right?"

Anna nodded, "Glynus…"

Pratt was already helping the other woman up. Glynus cried out when she tried to put weight on the ankle Anna had landed on. "It looks like you might have broken it," Pratt told her.

"Sorry," Anna said, wrapping her arms around the other woman.

Glynus shook her head and embraced Anna. "No. Don't ever apologize. You saved my life today."

Dresden handed a handcuffed and bleeding Frank Gilfer over to another officer and joined them. Frank had what looked like a bullet wound on his shoulder. Apparently, Dresden was a good shot. "That was smart, Miss Yesterday, throwing the blanket at him. He was distracted and he fired wildly. You probably saved our lives too."

Anna sniffed and swiped her cheeks. Now that the excitement was over, she was feeling shaky and sick to her stomach. She looked at Pratt. "Did Pierce get to you? Is he okay?"

"He did and he's fine. Last I heard he was cleaning the PD out of chocolate pudding."

She laughed, her teeth clacking together.

"We came as soon as we heard." Pratt favored Anna with a long look and then reached out, pulling her into his arms. "Come on, honey. Let's get you home."

"I want to go back to the store. Joss…"

He nodded, kissing her forehead. "Bill, I'm assuming our statement can wait until tomorrow?"

"Well, actually…" Dresden caught Pratt's raised eyebrows and sighed. "Okay. It's the least I can do. You take care of yourself, Miss Yesterday. I'll see you all at the PD in the morning."

"Thanks, Bill." Pratt started to lead her out but she stopped, looking at Glynus. "Do you want a ride to the hospital?"

Bill wrapped a blanket around Glynus's shoulders. "I got this, Anna. You go on home now."

Anna nodded and let Pratt lead her to the car, feeling as if she'd been beaten with a hammer for a few hours. Suddenly everything hurt.

***

"Buck was the one who broke into the antiques store and Frank Gilfer was responsible for all the rest?" Dresden's fingers were poised over his keyboard. He'd already taken their statements and was summing it all up.

Pratt nodded. "That's it in a nutshell. When Frank made the second blackmail call to Mason after Anna showed up with the clipping, Mason gave him an earful and demanded the article back. Gilfer knew he had a problem at that point so he forced Buck to help him get the news clipping from you. We all know how that worked out."

Dresden frowned. "But wouldn't the Mayor have recognized Gilfer's voice on the phone?"

"We think he used some kind of voice scrambler," Anna offered.

Pratt nodded. "Buck wasn't able to find the clipping so he took something he thought might be valuable enough to make me hand it over." Anna frowned. Joss still hadn't shown up and that bothered her.

"But Buck wasn't willing to just go along quietly, so he confronted Theodore Miller and learned what the story was about. Buck convinced Miller to give him his notes and the marked-up copy he'd saved all these years as security and Buck hid them in his basement office. Then Buck went to Mason but Perry Reese wouldn't let him in to see the mayor. He told Reese he was in trouble and the trouble was going to spread to Mason if they didn't help him. From what Anna told me, Reese told him to take a hike."

"And he showed up dead shortly afterward." Dresden frowned. "Gilfer apparently saw him leaving the mansion and determined that he'd told Mason who was behind the blackmailing."

"But if that were true, killing Buck wouldn't save Gilfer's blackmailing scheme," Anna offered.

Dresden shook his head. "No, but framing Mason for Buck's murder would. Gilfer figured he'd get as much as he could from Mason and then scamper, just like he told you. He had a one-way ticket to the Cayman Islands in his office when we picked him up."

Anna looked at Pratt. "And Gilfer came to Glynus's house yesterday hoping to find the copy Buck got from Miller?"

Pratt nodded. "He'd beaten the location of the evidence out of Miller and left him for dead. You and Glynus just got in the way. If you hadn't been there, he'd have just grabbed the copy and left."

Another piece of the puzzle sank into place in Anna's mind. "I just realized who attacked us at Quality. It was Gilfer wasn't it? He must have followed us that night. I remember smelling vinegar when he put his hand over my face, and you said there was vinegar on the tie that strangled Buck. What's with the vinegar anyway, he didn't strike me as a vegetarian."

Pratt laughed. "Gilfer had a bandage on his finger when I saw him at the hardware store. He told me he was trying a natural remedy for a wart. When I was a kid my mom used to put vinegar on our warts to get rid of them. It works pretty well."

"So that's how you knew it was Gilfer?" Dresden laughed. "And I thought the killer had just dribbled some of his lunch on his tie." He shook his head. "You know, you're too good a cop to give it up, Pratt."

Pratt shrugged Dresden's comment off but Anna, watching him closely, thought she saw something like regret flickering through his gaze. "That part of my life is over."

She wished she knew what had made Pratt change his life so completely. In fact, she realized in that moment there were a lot of things she wished she knew about the newest man in her life. "Well, I, for one am glad he's right where he is. I couldn't have gotten through this without him."

Pratt's cheeks reddened with embarrassment. "Are you done with us?" he asked Dresden.

"For now, yes. If I come up with any more questions I know where to find you."

"Yes," Pratt said, leveling a heated look at Anna, "you certainly do."

EPILOGUE

"What do you mean you can't get out?"

Joss crossed his arms over his chest and glared at the heavily painted specter sitting across from him. "I mean, I can project from the darned thing for a few minutes, but I can't work up enough gumption to appear to Anna or nobody else."

Bess frowned. "Whatever did you think you were doin' anyway, possessin' that savagerous critter?"

"I dunno. I reckon I was in a pucker, what with bein' locked in that rat hole and all. Don't get all grum, Bessy girl. I'm gonna find a way out o' this foul-tempered varmint if I have to create a full-blown spectral event to do it!"

His image started to fade and Bess stomped her foot. "Josselin Zebediah you're a right bastard! Don't you dare leave me here all by myself."

"It don't help getting' all wrathy, g'hal." Joss frowned at her, his handsome form flickering. "I'm workin' on extrapolatin' myself from this cursed critter. In the meantime, I need you to help me look after Anna. She tends to grab the little end of the horn on a reg'lar basis."

Bess crossed her arms over her abundant chest, scowling. "I ain't liftin' a finger ta help that dunderhead. You just need to get some grit and extrapolate yourself now!"

He faded to almost nothing and Bess gave a little cry, reaching for him as he popped away, leaving only his final words behind for her to cling to.

I'm comin' back Bessy, girl. Y'all keep things right and tight until I do.

THE END

ABOUT THE AUTHOR

USA Today Bestselling Author Sam Cheever writes mystery and suspense, creating stories that draw you in and keep you eagerly turning pages. Known for writing great characters, snappy dialogue, and unique and exhilarating stories, Sam is the award-winning author of 80+ books.